# SINS OF
# THE FATHER

DISCARD

# Norah McClintock

# SINS OF THE FATHER

Cover art by
## Laura Fernandez & Rick Jacobson

# Scholastic Canada Ltd.
Toronto, New York, London, Sydney, Auckland

**Scholastic Canada Ltd.**
175 Hillmount Road, Markham, Ontario, Canada L6C 1Z7

**Scholastic Inc.**
555 Broadway, New York NY 10012, USA

**Scholastic Australia Pty Limited**
PO Box 579, Gosford, NSW 2250, Australia

**Scholastic New Zealand Ltd.**
Private Bag 94407, Greenmount, Auckland, New Zealand

**Scholastic Ltd.**
Villiers House, Clarendon Avenue, Leamington Spa,
Warwickshire CV32 5PR, UK

**Canadian Cataloguing in Publication Data**

McClintock, Norah
 Sins of the father

ISBN 0-590-12488-9

I. Title.

PS8575.C62S56 1998     jC813'.54     C98-931054-X
PZ7.M33Si 1998

Copyright © 1998 by Norah McClintock

5 4 3 2 1          Printed in Canada          8 9/9 0 1 2/0

**Other books by Norah McClintock:**

*Shakespeare and Legs*
*The Stepfather Game*
*Jack's Back*
*Mistaken Identity*
*The Body in the Basement*

# Chapter One

"Where are we going?" Mick must have asked the question a hundred times. That and, "What's the big rush?" He might as well have been speaking Latin to a newborn baby for all the good it did. Dan didn't answer. All he'd say was, "Hurry up. We've gotta get out of here and we don't have all day."

So Mick threw jeans and T-shirts, clean socks and extra underwear, a sweater and his jacket into a nylon gym bag. Then, when Dan wasn't looking, he slipped in the little tin box of keepsakes he'd dragged with him wherever he went over the past six years. He zipped up the bag and allowed himself to be hustled out of the cramped apartment.

Whatever was up, there was at least one bright spot, Mick decided as he watched Dan lock the door of their apartment. The relentless, all-pervasive smell of pepperoni and tomato sauce from the pizzeria downstairs had killed his appetite — murder in the first degree. It would be a relief to get away from that.

"Just give me a hint," Mick said. Dan nudged him toward the back stairs. "Are we leaving the city?"

No answer.

"Are we making a run for the border?"

Nothing.

Well, that figured. It was Dan he was dealing with, after all. Still, a guy had a right to know where he was being spirited away to, especially when it was in such a rush. He also had a right to know why Dan had acted so spooked while he checked to make sure the gas was off and the coffee machine unplugged. He had jumped at the sound of every footstep in the hallway, every slam of a car door in the street below.

Dan threw Mick's gym bag into the trunk of the rusting old Chev he'd bought for a few hundred dollars from the owner of the garage where he worked. He waved Mick impatiently into the passenger seat and slammed his foot down on the accelerator before Mick could even buckle his seatbelt.

"Good move," Mick said. "Get yourself nailed for speeding before you go two blocks. Even I drive better than that."

Dan gave him a sharp look. "And just when have you been driving? You're not even sixteen — "

"In two months I will be."

"Then in two months you can criticize," Dan said. "Until then, I think I can manage without any backseat drivers."

Mick made a face. "I don't suppose," he said,

"that we're going to the airport to catch a plane and that by this time tomorrow we'll be surfing off Maui or snorkelling in the Gulf."

"I told you, we have to get out of town for awhile," Dan said.

"Okay. So *we* have to get out of town for awhile. What did *we* do? We didn't land ourselves in some kind of trouble again, did we?"

Dan shot him a sour look as he headed for the parkway. "You really should get that mouth of yours under control," he said. "It can get on a person's nerves."

"Is that why *we're* speeding?"

"Look, I can't explain the whole deal to you now," Dan said. "But it shouldn't be for more than a few days. A week at the most."

And that's all he would say. Mick settled back against the cracked vinyl of the car seat and wondered why he'd expected anything different. Dan was a jailbird, after all. Daniel Standish, his father, had been in prison when Mick was born.

"It's not Dan's fault," Mick's mother always told him. "He didn't do anything. It was all a mistake."

Maybe it was, Mick thought — the first time. But within six months of being released, Dan was serving time again. Altogether he'd done three stretches. For all Mick knew, this flight into the unknown was the lead-up to prison sentence number four. Staring out the car window, watching cars and buses and big rigs fly past them on the parkway, Mick told himself the same thing he always did when it came to Dan: I don't care.

Dan was a screw-up, the worst father in the world. Four months ago, when he'd been released again, Mr. and Mrs. Davidson — Bruce and Janine, as they liked Mick to call them — looked even sadder than he had when they heard the news.

"Maybe it'll work out this time," Janine said. She was a small woman with freckled arms. When she smiled, which she did often, Mick felt warm and welcome and safe. "You know what they say, three times is the charm."

"And if it doesn't work out . . . " Bruce said. "I'm not saying it won't, mind you, he's your father, Mick, and I know he loves you — but if it doesn't work out, you'll always have a home with us. You know that, son, don't you?"

When Bruce Davidson said 'son,' Mick's heart ached. Bruce was like a TV dad. You could count on him for a game of catch, a drive to early morning hockey practice, a man-to-man talk about grades or girls.

"I know," Mick said.

He'd cried when he left the Davidsons. He'd never cried when he was separated from Dan. For the past four months, Mick had been holding his breath, waiting to see if Dan would cross the line again so that Children's Aid would have to be called and Mick would be resettled into the back bedroom of the Davidsons' house in the west end. Half the time he hoped it would happen. The other half, he wasn't sure.

So far Dan had kept out of trouble. So far he'd held down a steady job as a mechanic at a busy garage ten minutes from the apartment. And so far he'd stayed off the booze. He came home every night to cook supper, and after he washed up, he took Mick out for ice cream or a movie or to throw a football around. It was almost as if he was actually trying, this time.

Suddenly Mick was hurled sideways as Dan tramped on the gas pedal and cranked the steering wheel, sending the Chev sideways across four lanes of traffic onto an off ramp. Mick cursed under his breath and fingered the frayed seatbelt that had held him in place.

"Ever heard of signalling a lane change?" he muttered.

But Dan wasn't listening. He was hunched over the steering wheel. His eyes flicked to the side and he jerked the wheel again, as abruptly as before. This time, though, Mick saw the move coming and braced himself. They were off the highway completely now and heading north on a two-lane road. Dan drove the next few kilometres with his eyes fixed more on the rearview mirror than on the road ahead. Then, after a nod — at *what?* Mick wondered — he made a few more sharp turns and headed back to the highway.

"What the — " Mick started, then clamped his mouth shut. What was the point of asking when you weren't going to get an answer? The plain truth was that maybe, despite appearances, Dan *wasn't* trying to go straight. Maybe right this minute he was taking another wrong turn. Mick wasn't sure how he'd feel if that happened — glad to get back

5

to the Davidsons, or like a fool for ever making that promise to his mother, and just plain stupid for believing, even for a moment, that Dan might actually care about him enough to keep his butt out of trouble this time.

Don't think about it, he told himself as the concrete highrises and the treeless subdivisions finally gave way to fields and farmhouses, barns and silos. Don't think about it. Hope for nothing and nothing will disappoint you.

"Can't you even give me a hint where we're going?" Mick said. "If *we're* taking a vacation, *we'd* sure like to know what to expect."

They were cruising down the highway, headed east.

"We're going to the farm," Dan said, as if there were only one, whereas when Mick looked around him, there seemed to be dozens.

"*The* farm?"

"Haverstock," Dan said.

Well, Dan had finally done it. He had surprised Mick. "You mean, where Mom was from?"

Dan nodded. "Your mother and me both."

This time when Dan didn't say anything else, Mick didn't mind so much. Whatever was going to happen, at least it would be interesting. Mick had never been to Haverstock before, even though he had relatives there. Now, finally, he was going to find out what it was about the place that made his mother turn white at the sight of its name printed on a postmark. Maybe he'd even find out why she'd once told him that nothing could ever make her go back there, not the promise of a million dollars, or a loaded gun pointed directly at her heart. He settled back in his seat, closed his eyes, and instead of pestering Dan with more questions that probably wouldn't get answered anyway, he fell asleep.

Mick woke with a jolt as soon as he realized that the car had stopped moving. His nostrils filled with a pungent fragrance. What was that smell? Something old? Something rotten? Something dead? Maybe all three. He blinked in the bright sun and tried to focus on the two men standing in front of the Chev, which was now parked on a U-shaped drive in front of a tiny grey-shingled bungalow. One of the men was Dan, tall and rangy in his black jeans and T-shirt. The other, the one Dan was talking to, was just as tall, but he was thick around the middle and had silver hair. An old man. A surly old man. He scowled at Dan, then squinted hard and fierce at the Chev as Mick unfolded himself from the front seat.

"What makes you think you can just cruise on in here asking for favours?" the old man said, spitting the words at Dan.

Dan swung away from him back toward the car. For a minute, Mick thought he was going to climb in behind the wheel and take off, but he didn't. Instead he circled around to the trunk and retrieved Mick's gym bag. He carried it to where the old man was standing and dropped it at his feet.

"Believe me, if I had any choice, I wouldn't be here," Dan said. "It won't be for long. A couple of days." He turned to Mick and waved him over. "Come on, Mick, there's someone I want you to meet. This is your grandfather, Big Bill." Then, to the sour old man, "Like it or not, Pop, he's your grandson. You going to turn your back on him, too?"

The old man scowled at Dan a few seconds longer before turning his attention to Mick. His pale old eyes studied Mick, and he nodded curtly.

"He's yours alright," was all he said.

"A couple of days," Dan said, "that's all I ask." He moved back toward the car, his car keys dangling on a ring from his finger. Before Mick realized what was happening, Dan was inside the car, turning the key in the ignition.

"Hey, wait a minute," Mick yelled. He ran toward the Chev. "No way are you leaving me here."

"It's just for a couple of days, Micky," Dan said. "I'll be back to get you as soon as I can."

Mick glanced over his shoulder at the sour old man. He couldn't stay here. The old goat looked like he'd murder Mick in his sleep.

"I'm *not* staying," Mick said. He wrapped his hands around the driver's side mirror to make his point.

Dan shook his head slowly. "You have no choice on this one, kid." He pushed down on the accelerator and the car leapt forward. Mick's arms were almost wrenched from their sockets; the mirror slipped from his grasp. "A few days," Dan called to him as he pulled back out onto the road. "A week at the most. I promise."

Then, in a cloud of dust from the gravel shoulder,

he was gone. Mick turned back to the old man, who looked like he was sucking on a dozen lemons all at the same time. Never, Mick told himself. I will never trust Daniel Standish again. Not if I live to be as shrivelled as that old goat. Not for a million dollars. Not even if a loaded gun was aimed directly at my heart.

Big Bill Standish wasn't Mick's idea of a kindly old grandfather thrilled to pieces to make the acquaintance of the grandson he'd never laid eyes on. If anything, he seemed angry as he watched Dan's rusty black Chev shoot down the road. He squinted after it until it disappeared from sight. Only then did he turn back to Mick. His expression hadn't sweetened any. He scowled down at the black gym bag on the gravel at his feet, then, his voice bitter, he said, "Well, I guess you'd better bring your gear inside."

He turned and trudged up the driveway to the house. Mick grabbed the gym bag and trotted after him.

Big Bill's house didn't look substantial enough to contain a man of his large build. It had an L-shaped combination living room and dining room. A stone fireplace dominated one of the living room walls. The mantlepiece was thick with framed photographs. Mick looked but couldn't identify Dan in any of them. Through the dining room, Mick saw a tiny kitchen. Besides that there were two small bedrooms, one at the front of the little house, one at the back, and a bathroom. The

9

old man didn't steer Mick to a bedroom or invite him to make himself comfortable in one of the living room armchairs. Instead he went straight to the phone, dialled a number, said exactly five words to whoever answered at the other end — "You'd better get over here" — and hung up. While he waited for whoever he'd called to appear, he examined Mick again. Mick could tell he didn't like what he saw.

Just as Mick was about to start squirming, he heard footsteps, and the door to the little house burst open. The man who entered the room took one look at Mick and uttered a few choice words that Mick's mother would never have tolerated.

"Dan was here," the old man said.

The newcomer, a stocky middle-aged man who looked vaguely familiar, stared at Mick with renewed interest.

"Danny? He was here? When?"

"A few minutes ago. He dumped the kid on me and took off."

Mick bridled under the choice of words. The old man made it sound like he was a bag of garbage.

The newcomer circled Mick warily.

"What's your name, son?" he said, his voice gentler than the old man's.

Mick told him.

The man shook his head, as if he wasn't sure what to make of the news. "Pleased to make your acquaintance, Mick," he said at last. "I'm your Uncle Jim." When Mick didn't immediately nod his understanding, Uncle Jim said, "Sounds to me like your folks didn't waste much breath on us, am I right?"

"I knew I had relatives here," Mick said. These guys seemed to like the direct, no-holds-barred approach. At least, they liked dishing it out. Mick decided to see how well they could take it. "But, no, Mom never talked about you. She said there wasn't a person in this town worth wasting her breath on."

If Uncle Jim was insulted, he didn't show it.

"Your mother was never one for keeping in touch," he said. "Your dad neither. So what made him suddenly change his mind and bring you here? Is it what Big Bill says? Is Danny trying to dump you on us?"

"No!" Mick said. It felt funny to be defending Dan, to be getting angry on his behalf. But he couldn't go along with what they were saying without making himself look bad, like he couldn't take care of himself, or like he'd let himself be suckered by Dan. "He had something he had to do. He's going to be back in a couple of days."

The two men exchanged glances. Uncle Jim looked down at the black gym bag on the rag rug in the middle of the floor and said, "That yours?" When Mick nodded he scooped it up and said, "Well, come on then. We'll get you settled in."

Mick followed his uncle out of Big Bill's house and across a yard as big as a field to a squat stone house on the far side of a row of cedar trees.

"The girls can bunk together. You can have Lucy's room," Uncle Jim said as he took the steps up to the back porch two at a time. "I don't suppose it'll kill them to have to share a room for a few days."

A woman standing at the stove in the kitchen turned when the back door opened. She took one look at Mick, gave a little cry, and immediately dropped the pie pan she had been holding. Blueberry filling splattered everywhere.

Uncle Jim let loose with a few more words Mick's mother would never have allowed. "Don't mind your Aunt Charlene," he said. "That's just her way of saying pleased to meet you."

A red-faced Aunt Charlene looked up as she swiped with an old dish towel at the mess she had made. "He looks just like . . . "

" . . . his father," Uncle Jim said. "This is Dan's kid."

Aunt Charlene's face went from red to white. "Dan?" she said. "Dan's here?"

"*Was* here," Uncle Jim said, his calmness a sharp contrast to Aunt Charlene's anxiety. "Mick's going to be staying with us for a couple of days, Charlene. I'm going to put him in Lucy's room, and then I bet he'd like something to eat, wouldn't you, Mick?"

Mick's stomach rumbled. It was way past lunch time, and he hadn't had a bite to eat since the cruller and coffee Dan had thrust at him when he dragged him out of bed shortly after dawn. He nodded.

"Afraid we'll have to pass on the pie, though," Uncle Jim said with a grin.

Mick trotted after him up the stairs. He didn't

know what had spooked his aunt, but he sure wished it hadn't. That pie had smelled good.

The sturdy stone house was filled with people by the time Mick had washed, run a comb through his hair and gone back down to the kitchen. Besides Uncle Jim and Aunt Charlene, there were two girls, both a lot younger than Mick. Big Bill was there, along with another man and woman, and a couple of boys — well, men, really, they looked to be at least eighteen or nineteen. Uncle Jim took charge and rhymed off everyone's names: cousins Lucy and Penny. Uncle Buddy and Aunt Anne and their sons Andy and Peter. They all watched as Mick tucked into the fried chicken and potato salad that Aunt Charlene set before him.

"So Danny was here, was he?" Uncle Buddy said. "He came, dumped his responsibilities on us and took off, is that about the size of it?"

"You couldn't get a better fit," Big Bill said. "The question is, what are we going to do with him?"

The adults all looked at Mick for a moment, which made him feel foolish. He'd been famished and had torn into Aunt Charlene's chicken. A bit of chicken skin was stuck to his chin. He wiped it away with a paper napkin.

"You don't have to do anything," he said. "Dan said he'd come back and he will."

Uncle Buddy peered at him as if he were an alien. "You don't know your father very well, do you?"

"Of course he doesn't," Uncle Jim said. "Danny's

spent more time in prison than out in the past fifteen years." He smiled kindly at Mick. "Don't worry. We'll do what has to be done. We'll take care of you."

Mick set down the chicken bone he had been holding. "I can take care of myself," he said as calmly as he could manage. It was clear these people didn't like Dan. It was equally clear that they resented Mick's presence. Well, that was a two-way street. Mick didn't want to be here any more than they wanted to have him. "Give me bus fare back home, and I'll be out of your hair today," he said to his Uncle Jim.

Uncle Jim laughed and started to fish in his pocket for his wallet. But Aunt Charlene, her eyes wide, grabbed his wrist so that it never cleared his Levis.

"You'll do no such thing," she said. "Be nice to the boy, Jim." She was clutching his arm with both hands, almost begging him. "You know it's not his fault."

Uncle Jim shook her off, like a big dog shaking off a pesky puppy. He laughed again. There was something phoney about the sound, but Mick couldn't figure out what.

"You're welcome here, Mick," Uncle Jim said. "A couple of days, a week, a month, it makes no difference to me. You're family."

Mick looked first at his uncle, then at his aunt. Something was going on here, but he told himself he didn't care what it was. He didn't know these people, and from what he'd seen so far, he was sure he wasn't going to like them. But without money, what choice did he have? He'd give it a day, maybe two, then, if he had to, he'd hitch back home and worry about what to do next once he got there.

The scent of chicken swirled around him. His aunt sure was a good cook, almost as good as Janine Davidson. Another day or two wouldn't kill him. Mick reached for another piece of chicken.

# Chapter Two

Mick lay between the crisp pink sheets of his cousin Lucy's bed and peered out the window at the moon that hung above the roofline of the barn. On his chest sat a metal box, once filled with chocolates, now containing his small hoard of keepsakes. Its lid stood open.

Mick fingered its contents. A cameo brooch that had belonged to his great-grandmother, and which his mother had worn on special occasions — for parole hearings and meetings with lawyers. A pair of pearl earrings in delicate gold settings. A woman's wristwatch with a worn leather strap. A small black bottle that once held his mother's favourite perfume, its scent now all but faded. One of these days when Mick unscrewed the cap, there would be no fragrance left to remind him of his mother's face, her soft skin, her gentle smile.

He sifted through a dozen photographs — his mother when she was young, his mother and father together before they were married, Mick and his mother when he was small, Mick in denim overalls, his mother in a waitress uniform. A slim bundle of letters, tied with string, most of them in long legal envelopes. Three of them, which had arrived after his mother's death, were a mystery. The envelopes were addressed in a bold black hand, and had no return address. All three were postmarked Haverstock. Each contained an uncashed money order for fifty dollars.

*A memory ... Mick is small, six or seven. He runs down the two flights of stairs to the little bank of mailboxes at the bottom, and pulls a few envelopes from the box labelled Standish. Most are bills. One is not, and his heart seizes when he sees the big black letters that spell out his mother's name. His mother frowns whenever one of these envelopes arrives. She never opens it right away, but sets it on top of the fridge, out of sight, and for the next few days, sometimes for as long as two weeks, she doesn't touch it. But eventually, always, she reaches for it. Her eyes are sad when she hooks a fingernail under the flap and runs it along the length of the envelope, slitting it open. She stares at the contents for a few moments before tucking it into her wallet.*

Now, lying on his cousin Lucy's bed and staring out into the past, Mick picked up the bundle of envelopes and held it to his nose, breathing deeply. But it had been too long. Nothing of his mother remained. He'd always wondered who had sent her the money. Uncle Jim, he now decided. Uncle Jim wasn't as hard as the rest. Or maybe Aunt Charlene, her pale eyes perpetually clouded with worry.

Maybe she'd fretted enough about Mick's mother to want to help her. It sure couldn't have been Uncle Buddy, a house of a man who'd gone on and on about how it was just like Danny to dump all his problems on someone else and not even stick around long enough to say thank you, not that anyone was likely to tell him he was welcome.

Big Bill was even worse. "Danny was always one to pass the buck," he'd said with disdain. "He never owned up to a mistake, never took responsibility for anything."

Aunt Anne, Uncle Buddy's wife, hadn't cracked a smile the whole time she watched Mick eat. She hadn't said a word, either, that Mick could remember, just scurried about, pouring cups of coffee for her husband and Uncle Jim and Big Bill, even though it wasn't even her house.

Aunt Charlene was quiet, too. Every time Mick looked up, she was staring at him. Staring at him and looking like she was seeing a ghost.

Mick hoped Dan hadn't been lying to him. He hoped Dan would come back soon, because no way could he hack it here for long. But he couldn't help wondering — what if all these new-found relatives were right? What if Dan *had* dumped him here like a load of garbage? What if he wasn't planning to come back?

Mick woke to the smell of bacon, eggs and coffee and the sound of children squealing outside. Bleary-eyed, squinting against the brilliance of the morning sun, he stumbled from his bed and staggered to the window. Down in the yard, running and shrieking, were his two cousins, Lucy and Penny. They were making as much noise as a whole schoolyard of first-graders. Mick had always heard that girls weren't as active or noisy as boys, but judging from the two wildcats chasing each other around a planter full of geraniums, that didn't seem to be true. He struggled to focus on the clock on the dresser. Seven-ten. What were little kids doing charging around, making enough noise to raise the dead, at seven in the morning?

He dragged on his jeans, pulled a T-shirt over his head, shoved his feet into his sneakers, and went downstairs.

Aunt Charlene, at the kitchen sink, looked so startled to see him that for one horrible moment Mick thought she was going to drop the stack of plates she was holding into the soapy water.

"You're up early," she said.

"It sounds like I'm the last one out of bed," Mick said.

"You are. But we decided to let you sleep in. I'm sure you're not used to getting up at dawn to milk the cows."

That was for sure. He sniffed at the lingering scent of bacon and wondered how to go about broaching the subject of breakfast.

"Well, sit down," Aunt Charlene said, shooing him over to the table. "I'll make you something to eat. How do you like your eggs?"

Mick blinked. Did she mean it? Could he pick any kind of eggs he wanted and she really would make them just the way he wanted them?

"Fried?" he asked.

"Sunny side up?"

He grinned. "Sunny side up would be perfect."

She shook her head. "I can't get over it, you know. The likeness is so perfect it's eerie."

Likeness? What was she talking about?

"When I first saw you yesterday I couldn't believe my eyes. I thought I'd suddenly been transported back fifteen years. You look exactly like your father. Exactly."

Mick shrugged. "I don't really see it," he said. But it wasn't the first time he'd heard it. His mother had often told him the same thing.

While Mick was eating his eggs, with crisp strips of bacon and slices of buttered toast, Uncle Jim came in from the barn.

"Well, well, look who's up," he said, grinning as he poured himself a mug of coffee and spooned sugar into it. "You want to take a ride with me? I'll show you around the place."

Mick shrugged. "Why not?" He sopped up the last of the egg yolk with a crust of toast, then set his dirty plate into the sink.

Aunt Charlene seemed surprised. "Thank you," she said.

Mick followed Uncle Jim outside and across a paved road to a lane on the other side. Uncle Jim unlatched the broad chain-link gate, swung it open to let Mick pass, then latched it again behind him. They started up the lane together, Uncle Jim striding along as sure-footed as a goat, Mick stumbling in the tire ruts and, once, stepping into a still-moist cowpat. Wire fencing ran along both sides of the lane. In the huge field to the left a couple of dozen black-and-white cows stood grazing. The fields to the right were empty of livestock. Back beyond another length of fence, Mick saw that the land had been cultivated, and guessed that some sort of crop had been planted, although he couldn't tell from looking at it what it was.

"Smell that country air," Uncle Jim said.

Mick sucked in a lungful. Country air smelled an awful lot like manure.

"I bet you can't breathe air like that in the city."

It depended on the neighbourhood, Mick thought, and the time of year, and the day of the week in relation to the next garbage pick-up.

"The Standish family has been growing corn and beans, and raising cows around here, for generations," Uncle Jim said. "The land your Uncle Buddy farms was passed down to him by your grandfather. It's been Standish land for a hundred and fifty years." He sounded proud of this fact. Mick looked out over the expanse of field and wondered why anyone would want to plant themselves on a single patch of land for all eternity. Didn't the Standishes have any imagination? Didn't they have the urge to see what lay beyond the horizon?

"What about you?" Mick asked, more out of politeness than anything else. After all, land was land. It all looked the same to him — flat and scrubby and filled with cow poop. "Didn't you get Standish land passed down to you, too?"

Uncle Jim shook his head. He leaned on a fence post and peered out over the field that was dotted with cows.

"I worked hard for this piece of land," he said. "By the time I finished agricultural college, I was working three different jobs to get the down payment for it. Then I had to keep working at the cannery over in St. Paul so I could keep it. Those mortgage payments can kill you, and bankers don't make it easy on a farmer just starting out." He shook his head. "Most folks around here work pretty hard. You have to. Cows need to be milked twice a day every day of the week, and when the crops are ready to be harvested, you better be ready, too. But there's work, and there's work. Back then, when I was doing shifts at the cannery and trying to make this land pay off, I was going at it eighteen hours a day, seven days a week."

Mick gazed at the mangy fields and lazy cows. He thought about the farmhouse where Uncle Jim lived with his family. It wasn't big or lavishly furnished. It seemed to Mick that Uncle Jim had worked ridiculously hard only to end up no better off than a factory worker or a garage mechanic.

"Come on back here," Uncle Jim said, striding along so quickly down the lane that Mick had to run to keep up. "Back there, beyond that bush," Uncle Jim said, "there's something I want to show you."

The bush he referred to wasn't a single shrub, but a long windbreak of maple and elm and scrub that, at first glance, didn't seem very far away, but which took them nearly twenty minutes to reach.

Uncle Jim quickened his pace as he led Mick through the cool shade of the maple grove and out the other side. Mick wasn't sure what he'd been expecting — some kind of landmark, maybe, or a breathtaking piece of scenery — but he knew he hadn't been expecting more of the same: more stubbly field, greater expanses of cultivated land, more crops he couldn't identify.

"See that?" Uncle Jim said. "That's Cooper land. That's been in your grandmother's family for the best part of two centuries. It's mine now. I inherited it when your Grandmother Margaret died. That piece of land doubled my holdings, made it one of the biggest farms in Haverstock. Bigger even than your Uncle Buddy's, and that's saying something. Usually it's the oldest son who gets it all."

Mick nodded, but didn't know what to say. No matter how you looked at it, it was just an immense stretch of dirt.

"What about Dan?" he asked.

Uncle Jim looked up sharply. "What about him?"

"If you got your mother's land and Uncle Buddy got your father's land, what did Dan get?"

"The thing about land," Uncle Jim said, "is there's only so much of it to go around, and when it's all gone, well . . . " He shrugged. "With your dad, though, it never got to be an issue. He hated farming, for one thing. Loved cars and girls and good times. And a few other things came up first, if you follow me."

Mick followed perfectly. A few things. One thing in particular. Prison.

"I could be wrong," Mick said, even though he knew there was no chance of it, "but it sure seems like no one around here has a very high opinion of Dan."

Uncle Jim shrugged. "I know he's your father, Mick. But the truth of the matter is that Dan's never done much to make things easy for himself. The way he tells it, trouble follows him around. But there's plenty of people out here, some of them in this family, who see it differently."

"Like how?"

"Namely that Dan's a guy who goes looking for trouble. And that's not like looking for gold or diamonds, things that are scarce. There's more than enough trouble in the world for anyone who cares to find it. You father is one of those."

"And you don't think he's coming back?"

Uncle Jim looked straight at him. His eyes were pale blue, like Dan's, but where Dan's eyes were always dancing around, never wanting to settle, Jim's gaze was steady, frank, commanding.

"He's your father. What do you think?"

Back at the farmhouse, with lunch over and Uncle Jim back at his chores, Mick had nothing to do but hang around the house . . . and think about what his uncle had said about Dan. A man who went looking for trouble. That was true enough. Once a year, in spring, Mick's mother would dress him in his best clothes — grey flannel pants bought from a thrift store and neatly pressed, a crisp white shirt, a jacket or cardigan sweater, a pair of second-hand black leather shoes. She would pin her cameo brooch to the front of her best dress, usually one she had sewn herself, and off they would go to the prison, a forty-five-minute bus ride away. His mother would carry a hamper of chicken and salad, cake and lemonade, a feast to celebrate Dan's and Mick's birthdays, which were three days apart.

They went every year for nine years, though Mick remembered only a half dozen occasions. Once his father had sat the whole time at the picnic table opposite his mother, holding her hands in his, gazing at her face, oblivious to the food she had laid out. Another time he had spent the whole visit pacing up and down, chain-smoking cigarettes and railing against "them," which Mick later found out was the parole board. Except for one time near the end, these annual visits were the only times Mick ever saw his parents together.

Then, when he was in grade four, everything changed. There'd been a knock on the classroom door and a summons to the principal's office. In the office were the principal, a friend of Mick's mother, and a man Mick had never seen before. A child welfare officer, he later found out.

Marie, his mother's friend, was the first to speak. The moment and all of its details had never faded from Mick's memory: the tears in Marie's eyes, the tremor in her voice, the wad of tissues, damp and mascara-stained, that she twisted in her hand, and her exact words: "Oh, Mick, there's been a terrible accident."

A wall had collapsed in the small plant where his mother worked. She'd been badly hurt — crushed, Mick was to discover much later — and had been rushed to the hospital. Mick was to stay with Marie "for now," the child welfare officer said. The two words made Mick tremble. "And then?" he had wanted to ask, but he hadn't dared.

Three days later — only two days before Mick's mother died — Dan appeared at the door to Marie's apartment, looking dazed, paroled at last. Released, it turned out, barely in time to say goodbye forever to his wife.

With Dan out of prison, Mick went back to his own apartment. He remembered that clearly, too. He handed his apartment key to Dan, who unlocked the door and stepped inside as reluctantly as if he were stepping into a gas chamber. He stopped just across the threshold, blocking the doorway so that Mick had to wriggle by him, and even then he continued standing there, gazing around, seeming to drink in every detail. He didn't say a word. Mick was afraid he was deciding not to stay, that he was going to turn and run. Mick didn't want that to happen. He didn't like staying at Marie's place. She smoked one cigarette after another. Her breath, her curtains, the sheets she used to make a bed for him on the sofa all smelled of smoke. She was a bad cook. Her meatloaf was grey and tasteless. The milk she gave him smelled funny and tasted bad.

Mick waited while Dan peered around the apartment. After awhile, he tugged on his father's sleeve until Dan stumbled a little farther inside. Then

Mick darted around him and slammed the apartment door.

Dan made bacon-and-tomato sandwiches. He toasted the bread golden-brown and cut the tomato paper-thin. The bacon he crumbled over top was crisp and crunchy. It was one of the best sandwiches Mick had ever tasted. He sneaked a look at his father as he ate it, wondering how he could have spent so much time in prison and yet still be able to make a sandwich that tasted so good. When Mick had finished, Dan pulled a comb from his shirt pocket, ran it through Mick's thatch of black hair and said, "We'd better get to the hospital, don't you think?"

Mick grinned. Marie had refused to take him to visit his mother. "They don't like little kids hanging around there," she'd said. Instead, she visited Mick's mother while Mick was at school, and later passed along messages that didn't sound like anything his mother would ever say. "She wants you to be a brave little man," Marie said. "She wants you to listen to what I tell you and to be sure to drink your milk." Mick's mother had never called him a little man and she never cared whether he drank his milk or not. "Millions of kids all around the world grow up big and strong without ever touching a drop of the stuff," she used to say. Then she'd laugh. "Who ever heard of a dairy farmer's daughter who didn't like milk?"

Dan hailed a cab and they went to the hospital, where Dan demanded to know Lisa Standish's condition.

"And you are . . . ?" the grey-haired nurse at the nursing station asked.

"Her husband. This is our son."

The nurse peered at Mick over the rims of her silver-framed glasses. "Perhaps the little boy would like to wait in the lounge down the hall," she suggested. "I'm sure he'd be more comfortable there."

"He'd be more comfortable if he could see his mother," Dan said. "She's been in here three days. He hasn't seen her and he misses her."

Even later, after everything else that happened, Mick remained grateful for that one thing Dan had done for him. That visit to the hospital was the last time he saw his mother alive. He didn't like to think how he would have felt, how much he would have regretted, if he hadn't had that opportunity. He was sure he'd be feeling differently now if he hadn't seen her one last time, if she hadn't pressed her lips against his ear and whispered what turned out to be the last words she ever spoke to him, and if he hadn't made a promise to her, crossing his heart and swearing to keep that promise, no matter what happened.

Halfway through the afternoon Mick thought he would go crazy from boredom until Uncle Jim said, "I have to drive Lucy into town for choir practice. You want to come?"

Uncle Jim's use of the word "town," Mick decided, was mostly ironic. Town referred to a half-kilometre stretch of two-lane road that widened temporarily to accommodate diagonal parking spaces, and was bordered with cement sidewalks. Crowded on either side of four short blocks was the sum total of Haverstock's business section. At one intersection, facing each other like rival gangs, were four churches — Anglican, Presbyterian, United and, the largest, Roman Catholic.

Uncle Jim pulled up in front of the United Church to let Lucy out of the truck.

"I'll be back at four," he promised her. Then he turned to Mick and said, "I'm driving out to Harold McKee's to check out his new bull. You want to come?"

A mental picture flashed before Mick's eyes, spliced together from what he knew about his two uncles, and what he'd seen the previous afternoon, when Harold McKee and another farmer named Walter Something-or-other had dropped by in a Jeep Cherokee to tell Uncle Jim about the bull. An afternoon at Harold McKee's would be an afternoon in farmer heaven. A couple or more middle-aged guys just like Uncle Jim, sun-weathered like him, their faces red and ruddy below mid-forehead, making them look like genuine farm types. When they took off their hats there'd be that stripe of soap-white skin that constituted the upper halves of their foreheads. Almost made you wonder which half was painted on, the red or the white. They'd stand around for an hour or two, just like they'd done yesterday, and talk about what a potent animal Harold's new bull was and how the cows would all enjoy his attention — there'd be plenty of sly chuckles at that — and then the talk would turn to money: the price they were getting for their milk, the price the cannery was paying for their beans and peas this year, the price some old-timer up the road had been offered for his land by some real-estate developer. Fun for farmers, maybe, but not Mick's idea of a great time.

"No, thanks," he said. "If it's all the same to you, I'd like to hang out here, see what's what."

Uncle Jim looked at him and laughed. "You drive through here once and you've pretty much seen it all."

Mick said nothing.

Uncle Jim shrugged and dug in his pants pocket for his wallet. He pulled out a couple of bills. "In case you want to get yourself a Coke or something," he said. "I'll pick you and Lucy up at the church in two hours. Don't be late. Lucy's the kind of girl who doesn't like to be kept waiting. She's my daughter and I love her, but I pity the poor guy who shows up at her door one minute later than he said he was going to." Apparently this was supposed to be pretty funny, because Uncle Jim laughed. He was still laughing as he drove away.

Uncle Jim turned out to be right about Haver-stock. Four blocks and five minutes later, Mick felt sure he had seen it all.

There was Nieland's Groceteria, a small store that even Mick knew didn't get much more than emergency traffic. His Aunt Charlene and Aunt Anne had made the thirty-kilometre drive to Morrisville first thing this morning to buy their weekly groceries at the Supercentre there. There was a hardware store with dust-streaked windows and a dollar store that Uncle Jim referred to as a "five and dime." A wooden bench outside Mae's Coffee Shop served as the Greyhound bus stop. According to a sign in the window, Mae was the authorized ticket agent. Mick went into The Book Place to check out the magazines, and came out shaking his head. It should have been called The God Place — it was filled with versions of the Bible and picture books of Bible stories. He peered into the drugstore window, strolled past a hairdressing salon, a barber shop, a women's clothing store and a place that seemed to sell everything from jewellery to china. The video store, at least, seemed to be up to date and relatively secular. It was crammed with little boys drawn by the arcade games that ran along one wall.

Mick crossed the street and trudged back down the other side, past two gas stations, an Ontario Provincial Police office, a veterinary office, another restaurant — this one advertising a liquor license and air conditioning — and a hotel, which also boasted a licensed lounge and weekend entertainment: This Saturday, The Four Horsemen! A farm equipment lot with a bank right next door for convenient financing, and that was it. He was right back where he started, outside of Nieland's.

He swung around, intending to scoot back to the Coffee Shop to get himself something cold to drink, and found himself face-to-face with a woman who did what seemed typical for Haverstock women the first time they saw him — opened her eyes wide as if she were startled. But this one did more. She started to lose her grip on the two paper sacks of groceries she was carrying. Mick made a grab for one of them, but instead of accepting his help, the woman drew back from him.

"Mom!" cried a girl behind the woman. "That bag is going to — "

The groceries fell to the ground with a thud. The cardboard carton of eggs leaked gooey yolk and gummy white.

" — fall," the girl said, and sighed.

Mick looked from the eggs to the woman. What was her problem? Couldn't she see he was just trying to help? Why was she acting as if he were a purse-snatcher or something?

The woman paid no attention to the eggy mess at her feet. Her eyes remained fixed on Mick. The girl behind her looked perplexed. She bent down and started to put the spilled groceries back into the bag.

"You're him, aren't you?" the woman hissed at Mick. "I heard you were in town. You're his son. You look just like him!"

The girl glanced up. Her eyes, Mick noticed, were green. Deep mossy green. "Just like who?" she said. "Are you feeling okay, Mom?"

The woman turned on her daughter. "His father's the one," she said. "The one who killed your grandfather."

The girl dropped the last of the groceries back into the bag and stood up. She looked at Mick with frank curiosity.

No wonder Mick's mother had never wanted to

come back to this town, he thought. She'd told him often enough that his father had gone to prison unjustly. His case was like Reuben "Hurricane" Carter's, she'd said, or Donald Marshall's, innocent men, sent away for crimes they hadn't committed. What she hadn't said, what she probably thought he'd figure out for himself, what only now hit him — with the force of a tornado — was that for an innocent man to go to prison, there had to be plenty of people who believed he was guilty. People like this woman.

"You tell your father he's not welcome in this town," the woman said. Her voice was loud and shrill. She had such a tight grip on the bag of groceries she was still holding that whatever was inside was in danger of being crushed. "You tell your father if he ever dares set foot in this town, I'll — "

"You'll what?" said a voice behind Mick. Mick turned to face a second woman. She was tall and slim, and stood with her hands on her hips as she regarded the scene. "Leave the boy alone, Wanda," she said. "You're talking about things that happened before his time."

"His father's a murderer and everyone around here knows it," the woman, Wanda, cried. She was shouting now, attracting the attention of passers-by. "Dan Standish killed my father. He'd better watch it if he ever sets foot in this town again."

The tall woman nodded. "Maybe you'd better get along home, Wanda," she said.

The girl tugged at her mother's sleeve, but

Wanda moved only reluctantly to her car. It seemed to take forever for her to put her groceries in the trunk, get in, and drive away. Mick glanced around. A half dozen people had stopped to stare at him. The tall woman shook her head.

"What's wrong with everyone around here?" she said loudly. "Doesn't anyone have any of their *own* business to attend to?"

That did the trick. The small knot of people dissipated, leaving Mick alone with the woman. She smiled at him and said, "Mick Standish, I assume."

Mick nodded.

"I'm Sandi Logan." She held up a thumb and forefinger so that they were almost touching. "I came this close to being your mother."

# Chapter Three

Mick stared at Sandi Logan, and wondered what she was talking about. She was surprisingly good-looking for someone her age. True, there were little lines around her eyes, and more at the corners of her mouth, but she had the face of a woman who smiled a lot, and her skin was smooth and tanned.

Sandi laughed. "Your father and I were good friends," she said. "He proposed to me when we were in the second grade. Never made good on the proposal, though. By the time he hit fifth grade, he'd fallen head over heels for your mother. That turned out to be the love that was meant to be." She squinted at Mick. "You really do look a lot like him."

"So I've heard," Mick said.

She glanced up and down the street. "Is Dan here with you?"

Mick shook his head.

Her bright smile faded a little. "But he's out . . . I mean, he did — "

"He's out of prison again, if that's what you

mean," Mick said. "He's been out for awhile."

Sandi smiled. "That's good. I'm glad." She hesitated before speaking again. "I sure was sorry to hear about your mother. She was a terrific person."

Mick wasn't sure what to say. He didn't talk about his mother much, mostly because there weren't many people in his life who had known her and were interested in listening to him ramble on about her.

"So," Sandi said, "you must be here visiting the family. This is your first time in Haverstock, isn't it?"

Mick nodded. "Mom mentioned this place from time to time, but she never seemed to want to come back here." He realized as soon as he'd said the words that Sandi might be insulted by them. She didn't seem to be, though.

"I guess you can't blame her." She smiled sympathetically. "Well, I'd better get going. I've got a couple of quarts of ice cream in the back of the truck but they're not going to stay frozen if I stand here yapping all day. Is Danny . . . is your father going to come and get you?"

Mick nodded, even though he had his doubts.

"If he does, tell him I said hi. I live out at the old McGerrigle place now, but you can tell him not to let that discourage him. I grow corn and tomatoes for city people. Tell your dad he's invited to come and have supper with me before he leaves town. You're invited, too."

She flashed him a smile, then climbed into a pickup truck at the curb. Mick waved when she pulled out of her parking space. It was crazy, he thought, waving at a woman he barely knew. Waving, he realized, because, unlike everyone else in Haverstock he'd met so far, she hadn't cringed at the mention of his father's name. She hadn't made any cutting remarks. In fact, she actually seemed to have fond memories of Dan. What kind of sense did that make?

Mick sat on the steps of the church, waiting for Lucy. His dark T-shirt drew the sun. He basked in the pleasant heat and wondered: had his mother gone to this same church? Had she been in the same grade as Sandi Logan? Hard to imagine that if she'd lived, she'd be around Sandi's age . . . She had been only twenty-seven when she died. Mick was nine. For his whole life up until then, he had lived with his mother in a series of one-bedroom apartments, some of them located above stores or restaurants, others in seedy highrises in the less desirable parts of town. Once, for six months, they'd lived in government-subsidized housing, but Mick's mother didn't like it there, where all their neighbours were poor and so many of them seemed to have lost hope. His mother wasn't like that. She lived on hope.

On the first day of January in the year that she died, she tacked a brand-new calendar to the wall beside the refrigerator. She flipped to October and there, under a full-colour photo of a bright white Victorian house surrounded by the flame and gold leaves of autumn, she circled the number 13. October 13, the day Mick's father would qualify for mandatory release. Every evening that year she got out a red marker and drew a big X through the day that had just passed. Week after week, month after month, the calendar beside the fridge was a record of days served, days closer to the day Dan would return.

"I don't want you to be ashamed of your father," she'd tell Mick. "Sometimes things happen to people, things that aren't their fault. That doesn't mean they did anything wrong. You understand that, don't you, Mick?"

Mick would nod, because she seemed to want his agreement so desperately. Things happen. A kid at school finds out your father's in prison. He taunts you. He calls your father a jailbird. He chants, over and over, "You know what they say, like father, like son," until, what else can you do, you have to slug the kid, which results in you getting hauled into the principal's office and pulling a week's worth of detentions. You're not the kid who makes the trouble, but you're the one who gets into it. Things happen.

"Everything is going to be different when your father is home again," she'd say. She always said it that way — home again, instead of out of prison.

And she was right. Everything was different.

Dan got out, she died, and there was Mick, living with a stranger in a tiny apartment, surrounded by his mother's things: her clothes; the floral print cushion covers she sewed ("I can't afford a new sofa, but I can sure afford a few dollars for cushions.

They brighten up the place, don't you think?"); the silver hairbrush she used every evening, one hundred strokes, while Mick read to her from a thick volume of bedtime stories; a couple of perfume bottles that Mick buried in his sweater drawer and took out at night to smell. It was eerily different being in a place where everything reminded him of her, with a father he had never lived with before.

Dan drank a lot. Mick wasn't sure where he got the money, but he always seemed to be working on a bottle of something. Sometimes he was just a little unsteady, burning the toast or spilling the milk. Other times, in the evenings or late at night, he was noisily drunk. After Mick went to bed, Dan played the TV too loud. When Mick got up to ask him to turn the volume down — something he did only once — Dan turned away, refusing to look at him. Mick saw him raise his arm and knew he was wiping tears from his eyes and face. Dan drank and wept. Once he fell asleep with a cigarette in his hand and almost burned the apartment down. The sofa had to be thrown out. Then he was late with the rent and when the landlord came hammering on the door to demand payment, Dan yelled at him and grabbed him by the collar and threatened to throw him down the stairs. The landlord called the police. Charges were threatened but not laid. Mick grew wary in his father's presence.

One day when Dan had been drinking too much, Mick skipped school. What was the point of school when you felt as bad as he did and when you were sure you were never going to feel better? What was the point of dealing day after day with kids who hated you or made fun of you because your father had been in prison for your whole life? On that day, a woman from Children's Aid had come to the door. She said, in an overly calm voice like a kindergarten teacher disciplining a horde of hyped-up five-year-olds, that she wanted to ask Dan a few questions.

Dan threw her out. Or, more accurately, he tried to throw her out. He grabbed her by both shoulders and started to hustle her toward the door. She was a small woman, a lot shorter than Dan, but she had good traction. There was Dan, steering her, pushing her, shoving her so hard toward the door that sweat beaded up on his forehead. And there was the little Children's Aid worker, an immovable object, refusing to be pushed. She wriggled around to face Dan and said, "If you don't remove your hands from my person" — she actually said that, *my person* — "I'll have to report you."

"Report *this*," Dan said. He laid a hand on her face and shoved her hard, so that she reeled back through the open apartment door. Dan slammed the door after her and locked it. She pounded on it for awhile, then went away. Dan seemed to forget all about her, but Mick didn't. He was pretty sure that such a stubborn woman couldn't be got rid of so easily. Sure enough, a couple of hours later she was back with a court order to remove Mick from the household, and two policemen to back her up.

Mick was surprised at what happened next, and stayed surprised no matter how often he thought about it later. The little woman from Children's Aid stood in front of two burly police officers and demanded that Dan hand Mick over. Mick expected Dan to jump at the chance to get rid of him. After all, he and Dan were strangers to each other. Mick expected Dan to say, "Well, I tried," and then shrug while Mick was carted off by the gutsy little social worker.

But Dan didn't do that, not even when the two police officers stepped forward.

"He's my kid and my responsibility," Dan said. Shouted. "So why don't you all just butt out?" Which, of course, the police didn't like, especially coming from an ex-con who'd had too much to drink. They liked it even less when Dan took a swing at them, but seemed pleased to have an excuse to arrest him. In the end, the woman from Children's Aid got her way. Mick often wondered what would have happened if Dan had remained calm, if he hadn't swung at a police officer. But wondering about the past was useless. It was history, and like all history, it couldn't be changed.

Besides, that was when Bruce and Janine Davidson had entered his life. Or, rather, he'd been thrust into theirs. Until then, he'd never known what it was like to live in a normal family, with a mom and a dad who were together and happy. While he waited in front of the church for Lucy to come out and his Uncle Jim to pick him up, Mick wondered how long he'd have to sit in Haverstock before he ended up back at the Davidsons. A week? Dan had said he might be gone that long. Two weeks? Surely if Dan didn't come back in two weeks, his relatives would be more than ready to get rid of him.

But what if Dan turned out to be as good as his word for a change? What if he actually came back? What then?

Day three and life in Haverstock was starting to feel like life in hell: lots of miserable people poking and prodding at him, making him miserable, making him desperate for a ticket out. He thought about picking up the phone and calling the Davidsons collect. Then he thought about what that phone call would say about him: Mick Standish, loser. He believed his father, the poor sucker. He allowed himself to be dragged out here to the middle of nowhere, and dropped with a pack of strangers, and all on the strength of a promise by the biggest loser of them all, Mr. Trouble himself, Dan Standish . . . Another couple of days, he thought. He'd give Dan that much longer before he pinned a Kick Me sign on himself and went slinking back to the city.

Sunday morning Aunt Charlene, in a green dress, with a white straw hat perched on her head, packed Lucy and Penny, both in dresses, into Uncle Jim's pickup.

"Are you sure I can't interest you in joining us, Mick?" she asked.

"Yeah," Lucy said, "you could hear me sing. I'm doing the solo today."

Mick shook his head. He hadn't been to church

since he was a little boy, and he didn't feel comfortable starting in again now in a place where everyone knew Dan and hardly anyone seemed to like him. He went out to the barn instead, to see if there was anything interesting to do. There wasn't. He climbed a ladder up to the hayloft and lay down to enjoy the quiet. The next thing he knew, he was waking up to the sound of voices down below. Two of them. Uncle Buddy's and Uncle Jim's.

" . . . ship him back, that's what I'd do," Uncle Buddy was saying. "Only I wouldn't buy the ticket for him, I'd send him collect. Let Danny pick up the tab at the other end."

"And if Danny doesn't pay or isn't there to pick him up?" Uncle Jim's voice. There was a lightness to it, as if he were teasing his older brother. "Then what do you suppose they'd do? Stash the kid in the lost and found? Come on, Buddy. Whatever Danny did, it's not the boy's fault."

"Did I say it was?" Uncle Buddy said. "My point is, get rid of the kid and you get rid of the chance of Danny showing up here again. He's a troublemaker."

"C'mon, you think he's going to run someone else down?"

Mick sat up straight. What did Uncle Jim mean by that? Did it have anything to do with the screeching woman he had met in town?

"He could spill the beans to Charlene. I wouldn't put that past him. He'd probably find some way to use that against you, maybe even squeeze some more money out of you."

"I doubt it," Uncle Jim said. "That stuff's all water under the bridge."

"Is that right?" It was clear from Uncle Buddy's tone that he didn't agree. "So you're telling me that if Danny were to show up here and tell Charlene about that little fling you had with Helen Sanderson fifteen years ago, Charlene would just shrug and say, 'That's water under the bridge'? How long have you been married, Jimmy? Must be about five minutes if that's all you know about women."

Uncle Jim said nothing.

"Take the kid into town and buy him a one-way ticket home," Uncle Buddy said. "Get him out of here before Danny shows up."

"If Danny comes back — and I'm not saying he will, I don't think he's changed that much — but even if he were to come back, I don't think my mistakes are going to be on his mind," Uncle Jim said. "After everything that happened, I don't think even Danny would have the nerve to talk about someone else's sins."

"Too bad you didn't think like that back then. You could have saved yourself a lot of money."

"Back then I stood to lose a whole lot more if Charlene found out. But that was then and this is now. Come on. I don't know about you, but I could use a cup of coffee. Charlene tried out a couple more pie recipes this morning."

"She's serious about that contest, huh?"

"Serious? Got her heart set on winning that brand-new kitchen they're giving away as first prize. I already told her I didn't think the farmhouse of the past was any place for what those contest people are calling the kitchen of the future, but you know Charlene. So, how about it? You want a slice of warm apple-strawberry, or a peach cinnamon crumble? Or maybe some of each?"

Uncle Buddy's laugh was rich and greedy. Their work boots thumped across the barn's floorboards.

Slowly Mick stood up. Great, he thought. Not only did some people in this town — like that horrible woman in front of the grocery story — think Dan was responsible for a death. Now it turned out that his dear old innocent father was a blackmailer, too.

Sunday dinner. Jim and Charlene, Lucy and Penny, Mick and Big Bill, Buddy and Anne and Peter and Andy, all seated at the table in Aunt Charlene's dining room. Her best silver and china all laid out. Roast beef, roast potatoes, gravy, three kinds of vegetables, homemade buttermilk biscuits, a couple of pies sitting on the sideboard. Mick had never sat at a table so laden with food, but despite his hunger, he couldn't eat. Not with Big Bill going on and on about Dan.

It started when Aunt Charlene mentioned that Wanda Stiles had been "downright snippy" with her at church.

"She gave me dirty looks all through the service," Aunt Anne added. "You saw her, Buddy. Every chance she got, she glowered at me. Then after the service, there she was at the back of the church, staring. Well, I don't know who she thought she was dealing with, but I showed her. I marched right up to her and said, 'If you have something to say to me, Wanda Stiles, then you'd better come right out and say it.' And she did, too. What a nerve. She said, 'You tell that brother-in-law of yours that he'd better not show his face in this town.' She said it in a nasty tone, too, as if she thought she could scare me."

"She's crazy," Uncle Buddy said, with his mouth full of potato. "She hasn't been right in the head since the day her father died."

"She hasn't been right in the head since the day she was born," Uncle Jim said. "Remember her as a kid? Always dressed funny. Always had her head in those weird books. What were they? Magic books or some such nonsense."

"Books about the occult," Aunt Anne said. "I remember. She used to say she wanted to be a witch. A white witch."

"What the heck is a white witch?" Big Bill demanded.

"A witch who does good," Lucy said, and everyone turned to stare at her. Her cheeks reddened. "I read about it somewhere," she said defensively. "It's not like I am one or anything."

"Wanda Stiles is as sane as the next person," Big Bill said. "She just never got over the death of her father, and who could blame her? The man was mowed down in the prime of life. The McGerrigles and the Stileses used to be good friends of this family. They helped each other out for generations. Dan put an end to that." He stared down the table at Mick.

"Dan didn't do anything," Mick said automatically. He'd been saying it all his life.

Big Bill couldn't have looked more surprised if his old pal Barry McGerrigle had walked into the room, sat down at the table, and said, Pass the gravy.

"Is that what he told you?" Big Bill said. The sarcasm in his voice was as thick as the butter on his biscuit.

Mick stared evenly at his grandfather. What a sour, bitter, angry old man he was. He hadn't said one good thing about Dan — his own son — in the three days Mick had been in Haverstock. Mick was beginning to wonder if he'd said anything positive about Dan back then either, and whether, if the occasion had arisen, he would have fought to keep Dan the way Dan had fought to hold onto Mick that time, or whether he would have just handed him over to the authorities.

"That is what he told you, isn't it?" Big Bill said. "He's probably been moaning for years that it wasn't his fault. Nothing was ever his fault. You want to do yourself a favour, boy? Face the facts. Your father is a screw-up. Always has been, always will be. How long has he ever managed to stay out of jail? Three months? Four? Five at the most, I bet."

"Bill!" Aunt Charlene said. She looked horrified.

Four months, Mick thought. This time was the longest so far, and so far it was four months.

"And all that time he was behind bars, where were you, eh? Did he care what happened to you?"

47

What about *you?* Mick wanted to shout at the old man. Did *you* care what happened to me or my mother? Do you care now? But there was no point. He wanted nothing to do with this grizzled old fart, or with any of them rest of them. He just wanted out.

"What do you think your father's doing now, eh?" Big Bill said. "He brings you out here, dumps you on us. Why? You think he did that because he's gone and bought himself a suit and a tie and he's showing up every day at a respectable job? You think that's what's going on? I wouldn't be surprised if he was up to his neck in a manure pile right now. Why else would he have dropped you on us? He's probably gone out and done something stupid again, and if he isn't already in jail, he's probably hiding out somewhere with the police breathing down his neck. That's the thing about your father, isn't it, kid? He's not smart enough to keep himself out of trouble, and he's not smart enough to keep himself out of jail, either."

Mick stood abruptly, sending his chair shooting back across the room. He opened his mouth to speak, but what could he say? You're wrong? Dan isn't in trouble? Even if it wasn't true now, it was only a matter of time. Hadn't Big Bill just said out loud what Mick had been thinking? So why did it sound so bad coming out of the old man's mouth? Why did it make Mick's stomach churn to hear Dan's father say the very thing that Mick had been turning over and over in his own mind?

"Sit down, Mick," Uncle Jim said.

But Mick couldn't sit. Or speak. He turned and ran from the room. Behind him he heard Big Bill say, "Just like his father. At the slightest sign of the truth, he turns tail and runs."

Mick ran, all right. He ran out of the house and into the long summer night. He ran and he kept running. Nothing, he thought, could ever make him return to that house. Absolutely nothing.

# Chapter Four

Mick was in second grade the first time a kid gave him a hard time about Dan. "Your father's a killer," the kid said. Mick denied it, and used his fists to back himself up, but the kid wouldn't quit. "My father didn't do it," Mick said. "He shouldn't even be in there." He always called it that — "there," instead of "prison."

Since then he'd heard it all.

"The prisons of the world are filled with innocent people," Mr. Beton said. Mr. Beton was their landlord for awhile, until Mick's mother got tired of him coming around saying he had to check the wiring or the plumbing or the water meter, always ready with some excuse for why he was there and always staying a lot longer than he needed to, always staring at Mick's mother. "To hear them tell it, there isn't a convict in custody that deserves to be there — each and every one of them is the wrong man."

Or, from a kid in sixth grade, after Dan had been

sent back for parole violation: "If he was found guilty by a jury, then he's guilty. People who don't face up to what they've done are always blaming other people. They always screw up again and end up back inside. That's what my dad says." The kid's father was a cop.

Against them all was Mick's mother. "Your father would never intentionally hurt anyone," she said. "It's all a mistake, a terrible mistake. You have to believe that, Mick, no matter what anyone says. Promise me you'll believe in your father."

Mick promised.

"Promise me, Mick," she had whispered in his ear at the hospital that last time he saw her. She was bandaged everywhere — her hands, her legs, her head. Her face was so swollen he barely recognized her at first. Dan had to nudge him closer to the bed. She spoke with difficulty. There were long pauses between some of the words. "Promise me you'll stick up for your father. Promise me you won't believe any of the lies people tell you. Help him, Mick. Be proud of him."

She said it like it was a magic formula: Believe in him and everything will be fine. She didn't live long enough to see how wrong she was. Sure, Dan had been released, but he hadn't managed to stay on the street side of prison for long. He always got into trouble and always ended up back inside. Mick wondered what his mother would think if she were here now, if she could see how little all her believing had accomplished.

Dan's own father didn't believe in him. His

brothers didn't believe in him. The daughter of the man who had been killed sure didn't believe in him.

The daughter of the man who had been killed . . . by Dan. That's what everyone here said. Mick's mother had told him one thing all his life, and now everyone he met was telling him something else — that Dan Standish was a killer.

"Mick?"

The voice was so soft and came to him through such a sweet bath of sunlight that Mick knew he was home in his bed and that if he opened his eyes, he would see his mother smiling at him from the doorway, and she'd tell him to hurry up, breakfast was already on the table.

"Mick Standish, what are you doing in my barn?"

It wasn't his mother after all. It was Sandi Logan standing over him. And he wasn't home in his bed. He wasn't in a bed at all, but sprawled on a pile of hay. He sat up with a jolt and started to pour out a hundred apologies. Sandi held up a hand to silence him.

"You're saying sorry to the wrong person," she said, then she turned and shouted to someone Mick couldn't see. "Heck! Heck, I've got Mick Standish in here. Do me a favour, will you? Call Jim and let him know."

Mick heard something — someone — move in the distance.

"Far as I know," Sandy said, "Jim and Buddy and half the men in the area have been out looking for you since first light. How'd you end up here?"

"I don't know," Mick murmured. It was close enough to the truth. He had run without giving any thought to where he was going, or even where he could go. He had less than ten dollars in his pocket — not enough for bus fare home. He'd thought, I'll find a phone. I'll call Bruce Davidson. But out here finding a phone meant knocking on someone's door, and he was pretty sure that everyone in the area knew his uncles.

"Come on," Sandi said, stretching out a hand to him. "Up and at 'em." She was stronger than she looked, and hauled him to his feet as effortlessly as if he were a small child. "Let's take you inside and get some breakfast in you."

As he followed her across the yard, a grizzled old man came toward them.

"Heck, this is Mick Standish. Mick, this is Heck Dinsmore. He and I run this place."

Mick nodded in acknowledgement. Heck Dinsmore said nothing in reply, but stared at Mick through watery eyes.

"Jim says he'll be over directly," he said, then walked away without another word.

"Heck can be a little crusty," Sandi said. "Don't mind him." Then she called, "Breakfast'll be ready in ten minutes, Heck!"

Sandi's house was small but well cared for. Its bright kitchen was the largest room on the ground floor. Sandi sat Mick down at a big pine table and poured him a tall glass of orange juice. While he drank it, she started to work on breakfast.

"Pancakes okay?" she said.

Mick nodded. He loved pancakes. Nobody made them better than his mother.

"So, you going to tell me what happened?" Sandi said as she cracked an egg into a mixing bowl. "Were you running away, or did you go out for a midnight stroll and forget to go back home?" Her voice seemed light-hearted, but there was nothing amused about the look in her grey eyes.

He shrugged. "I got lost, that's all."

Sandi's eyes seemed to register the message: I don't want to talk about this. "I can see how that could happen," she said. "Up to a point. I mean, there was no fog last night, and we sure didn't have one of those big snowstorms that have been known to blow through here in winter, the kind that are so bad you can't see three feet in front of your face. True, you're a stranger and it does get a lot darker at night here than it does in the city, so I guess I could see how you might have got lost and made your way to my barn. But not to be able to find your way from the barn to the house? Sorry, Mick. I don't buy that."

He stared down into his juice. It shouldn't have mattered whether she bought it or not — she was nothing to him — but if it didn't matter, why couldn't he look her straight in the eye?

"Your Uncle Jim was pretty worried," she said. "He had your Aunt Charlene and your Aunt Anne making phone calls all over town to ask if anyone had seen you. That's why I was out in the barn. I don't have any animals, I just use the place for storage. I went out there looking for you, and what do you know?" She was stirring the pancake batter with a big wooden spoon. "Don't you have anything to say for yourself?"

"I'm sorry," Mick said, the two words guaranteed to restore peace and quiet. There wasn't an adult alive who didn't like to hear a kid admit he'd been wrong.

The back door clicked open, then clattered shut. Not Uncle Jim, he prayed. Not before the pancakes.

It was Heck. He entered the kitchen silently, poured himself a mug of black coffee, and sat down at the table.

The first spoonful of batter dropped with a hiss onto the hot griddle and kicked up a delicious aroma. What was that? Blueberries? Had she really put blueberries into the batter? Mick's mouth started to water.

"Were you headed home?" Sandi asked. She dropped a second spoonful of batter into the pan, then a third.

Mick shook his head.

"Just out for a little air, huh?" she said, and flashed him a smile.

He stared at her, baffled by her seemingly cheery expression.

"I know your grandfather," she said. "People around here say he's set in his ways. Some even go so far as to call him stubborn. He has strong opinions and isn't afraid to state them — over and over." She stacked the pancakes onto a plate, which she slid in front of Mick. "Butter and syrup are already on the table," she said. "Dig in."

While he poured syrup on his pancakes, she started another batch. Mick took a bite. Hot juicy blueberries burst in his mouth. He grinned. "These are great."

She nodded in acknowledgement and didn't speak again until she had served a stack to Heck, and seconds to Mick. Then she sat down at the table with a plate for herself.

"Jim should be here in a couple of minutes," she said. "Look, Mick, we don't really know each other. But I do know your family. I know how it can be sometimes. I want you to know that you're always welcome here. There's plenty of work that needs doing, and there's generally only Heck and me to do it. Anytime you need to get away, you can come over here, grab a hoe or shovel, and help me out. I'd probably be able to pay you something for your trouble. Not much, mind you. But something. And, who knows — "

"Knock, knock," said Uncle Jim from the door.

Mick's stomach cramped. He didn't realize how much he was dreading going back with his uncle until he heard that voice. He set his fork aside, leaving the rest of his pancakes untouched.

"Well, well," Uncle Jim said as he strode into the kitchen, "look who's here."

He wasn't alone. A tall man in an OPP uniform was with him.

"Hi, Jim, Les." Sandi smiled at both men and stood up. "Can I offer you two some coffee?"

"Not for me, thanks," the officer said. He stared at Mick for a moment. Then his eyes settled on

Heck, who stood up and carried his dishes to the sink, even though he hadn't finished what was on his plate.

"Not running out on us, are you, Heck?" Uncle Jim said.

Heck seemed to be doing exactly that. He squeezed by Jim and Les and hurried down the back steps. Mick saw him through the kitchen window a moment later, disappearing into the barn.

"That man has no gumption," Jim said as Heck disappeared through the barn door. "Never did. No wonder his wife gave up on him." He turned to Sandi. "I never did understand why you took him on as a partner, Sandi."

"Since when is my business any of yours?" Sandi said stiffly. Clearly she was not happy about Jim's attitude.

Jim threw up his hands in a gesture of surrender. "Okay, okay," he said. "I apologize. I guess you can't hold a man's past against him forever."

Can I get that in writing? Mick wanted to ask.

Sandi sighed. "You sure you won't have a cup of coffee? It's just made."

"No, thanks," Uncle Jim said. "I've been on the go for hours and I still haven't put a dent in my morning chores. And I'm sure Les has some crime that needs fighting, isn't that so, Les?"

Les laughed. "Oh yeah," he said. "There's probably some big case waiting for me right now. A stray cow, maybe. Or a dog wandering around town without a licence."

"More likely there's a chess game set up in your office and you want to get back there and ponder your next move," Sandi said. She caught Mick's baffled expression and explained. "Les and your Uncle Jim are chess fanatics," she said. "They've always got a game on the go. Who's winning this one, Jim?"

"Matter of fact, I am," Uncle Jim said. "Well, we've wasted enough time on this particular problem," he said, looking directly at Mick, waiting, Mick knew, for those magic words — I'm sorry — spoken humbly. This time Mick didn't speak them. "Your Aunt Charlene was worried sick," Uncle Jim went on. When Mick still said nothing, his uncle shook his head. "Come on, then," he said. "I'll show you how to shovel manure. I know it's something you've been dying to learn ever since you got here." He laughed and slapped Mick on the back.

Mick's mother had never told Mick exactly what had happened. She referred to it as "the accident." Or, "that night." She'd say, "It doesn't matter what they all say, he didn't do anything wrong." Mick had been made to understand that there had been a death, and that Dan had been sent to prison for it. Once, when he was six or seven and some kids at school had been giving him a hard time, he had screwed up his courage and asked, "Did he" — back then it was always "he," just as now it was always "Dan"; it had never been Dad or Daddy or even Father — "Did he kill somebody?"

His mother's face had turned as white as milk.

She struggled for composure. She sat Mick down on the rickety sofa in the living room, perched beside him and held his hands in hers.

"People will talk," she said. Her lips trembled. Her hands were cold on his. "People will say all kinds of things, even when they don't know what they're talking about. Your father shouldn't be in prison. He didn't do anything. He would never intentionally hurt another human being. It was all a terrible mistake that he's paid for ten times over. Do you understand me, Mick? Do you understand what I'm telling you?"

At the time what he understood was that his father was an innocent man, wrongly accused. A little later, however, after his mother died and Mick found himself trying to sleep over the racket of the television that was muffling the sound of his father's sobbing, Mick turned his mother's words over and over in his mind. Then, when it was too late to quiz her, he realized that she'd spoken always in code. Prison was "that place," the parole board was "those people," the circumstance that had sent his father to prison was "that terrible accident." She never spoke of the life that had been lost. It wasn't until he came to Haverstock that he was confronted with the results of that "accident," that he'd heard the word "killer" spoken. And still he had no clear idea what had happened. Neither his mother nor Dan had ever told him. Now, as he peered out the window of his cousin Lucy's bedroom, he realized that he would never be in a better position to find out.

He wandered out to the shed where his uncle was tinkering with the engine of his tractor. "If you don't need me around here," Mick said, "I'm going over to Sandi's for awhile."

Uncle Jim squinted questioningly at him. "What's she got that I don't have?"

"She offered me a job. She said she'd pay me."

Uncle Jim shrugged. "Guess I can't argue with that. Be back for supper, though."

"Tell me," Mick said to Sandi Logan. He was standing behind her while she hunted in a tool shed for some equipment for him. He'd told her he was there because he wanted to work — and he did. He could use some money, and so far she was his best prospect of getting any. But there was another reason he had returned to her farm. A more important reason. "Tell me what happened, everything you know."

Sandi frowned as she handed him a hoe, and glanced over at Heck, who was sitting in the shade of the barn, sharpening the blade of what looked like a pair of hedge clippers. Heck's face was impassive. Mick couldn't tell whether he had heard or not.

"Really, Mick," she said, "I don't think there's anything I can say that you haven't heard a hundred times. Surely your mother — " She broke off when he shook his head. "You were small. I guess she didn't want to . . . " Her voice trailed off.

Didn't want to what? Mick wondered. Didn't want to hurt him? Well, he *was* hurt — by his ignorance of something so important, and by the realization that perhaps his mother's silence wasn't the result of wanting to spare his feelings. Maybe she simply hadn't wanted to tell him the truth. Maybe she'd even lied to him to protect Dan and hadn't given a moment's thought to what that lie might mean to Mick. Maybe Dan was more important to her than Mick was. Either way, it didn't make much difference. It all came down to the same thing.

"Tell me," Mick said.

Sandi glanced at Heck again, then sat down on the back of an old wagon and motioned for Mick to sit beside her. Slowly she began to talk.

"Dan was down at the hotel that night," she said, "having a couple of beers. I know, because I was a waitress back then. I probably served four out of every five beers in Haverstock in those days, and I served Dan that night.

"It was a Wednesday, not especially busy. There were no more than a dozen customers. Dan was one of them. Barry McGerrigle was another. Barry was an older man, about the same age as your grandfather. He used to own this place. Back then, it was a going concern as a dairy farm. That summer Dan had done some work for Barry. Remember, your dad wasn't much more than a kid at the time, nineteen years old."

Mick nodded, even though he had never thought about it that way before.

"He was a wild thing. Your grandfather had a devil of a time keeping track of him — he was either sleeping late when he should have been up helping your uncle Jim or your uncle Buddy with the ploughing or the planting or the haying, or he was out late, driving your mother all over the county or drinking with his buddies. He'd calmed down a little, though, because your mother was talking marriage and, to everyone's surprise, Dan wasn't trying to talk her out of it. I think your grandmother was even hoping that Lisa — I mean, your mother — would be the influence that would finally make a solid citizen out of Dan.

"Anyway, he'd been working for Barry McGerrigle for most of that summer, and apparently there was a discrepancy between what Barry paid him for the work and what he had agreed to pay him. At least, that's what Dan claimed. Barry told it differently. Dan was stewing about that and had been for quite some time. He'd complained about the situation to just about everyone in town. He went around calling Barry a cheat. Barry didn't like that, although, to be honest, no one else seemed to have much objection to the label. Barry had a reputation. I don't want to say he was cheap, but I will say that he hated to let a dime slip through his fingers."

Mick allowed himself a smile.

"Well, Barry came into the lounge after Dan had had a few beers, and before I even served Barry his first drink, Dan was all over him, demanding his money, calling Barry names, telling him he knew perfectly well why Dan needed the money he was owed and Barry had better come through or else.

The two of them got into a bit of a scuffle . . . "

The barn door slammed, snapping the thread of Sandi's narrative. The clippers that Heck had been sharpening lay abandoned on the grass. Heck was nowhere in sight.

"Where'd he go in such a hurry?" Mick asked.

Sandi shook her head slowly. "Heck doesn't like to hear about this," she said. "Back then he was a regular down at the hotel. He was there that night. In fact, he joined in the fight. He had his own differences with Barry McGerrigle."

Mick raised an eyebrow, but Sandi went on without noticing.

"The truth is, a lot of people around here seemed to have a grudge against Barry. He was what we called a difficult character. So when Heck saw your father light into Barry, he jumped in himself. Some might say he egged Dan on. About the only positive thing to come out of the whole mess was that Heck stopped drinking. Sobered right up."

Mick nodded impatiently. He didn't care about Heck. He wanted to hear the facts. "So, you were saying?"

"It took a bit of convincing," she went on, "but I got Barry to leave and I called your Uncle Jim to come and get Dan, which he did. Jim got Dan out of the bar and into the parking lot, and I was just breathing a sigh of relief when I saw them start to fight over the car keys. From where I was standing, it looked like Dan didn't want Jim to drive. Dan'd had a few more beers than he should have and he was still hot under the collar about Barry not paying him. Anyway, the two of them were scuffling away out there. For a few moments, I thought it was going to come to blows. Then Dan said something — I couldn't hear what it was, of course, but whatever he said it took all the fight out of Jim. He threw the car keys at Dan. Dan laughed and climbed in behind the wheel. I could hear him rev the engine and he was about to tear out of there when all of a sudden Jim grabbed the passenger door handle and opened the door and jumped in. The car was moving before he even got the door shut. That's all I saw."

"But you must know what else happened," Mick prompted.

"All that I know about what happened after that is what I was told. They drove past Barry's place on their way home. Barry was out on the road with his dog. He was struck by Dan's car and killed. I guess you know the rest after that."

Mick had started to tremble when Sandi was halfway through her story. If he hadn't been sitting, he would have fallen down. His mother had always said Dan had done nothing wrong, but the way Sandi told it, it seemed that he hadn't done a single thing right that night.

"So you're saying Dan did it?"

Sandi looked down at the ground for a moment. When she looked back up at him, her eyes were filled with regret.

"The charge he answered to was manslaughter. I'm sorry, Mick. I thought your mother would have told you everything."

"What you're saying," Mick said slowly, "is that my father went out one night, got himself good and drunk" — Mick could picture it; there'd been plenty of times after the funeral when he'd seen Dan drink more than was good for him — "then he got into his car and ruined his own life, my mother's life and my life. Is that about the size of it?"

"Aren't you forgetting something?" said a voice behind Mick. He whirled around and stared into the moss green eyes of Wanda Stiles's daughter. "He also killed my grandfather."

# Chapter Five

"Jessie!" Sandi seemed as startled as Mick to see Wanda Stiles's daughter. "What are you doing here?"

"I work here, remember?" Jessie Stiles said. "What's *he* doing here?" She nodded in Mick's direction.

Sandi cleared her throat awkwardly. "He works here, too," she said.

Her apologetic tone stung Mick. It sounded like she was embarrassed to have him around. She was probably sorry she'd offered him a job. He thrust the hoe back at her. "Forget it," he said. "I'll clear out."

Jessie's cool green eyes studied Mick carefully. She took the hoe from Sandi and pressed it back into his hand.

"I know how much work there is to do around here," she said. "I also know how much Sandi needs the help, especially now. If you agreed to work for her, the least you could do is live up to that agreement. Right, Sandi?"

Sandi looked first surprised, then relieved. "Right," she said. "We made a bargain, Mick, a fair day's work for a fair day's wage. You're not going to back out on me, are you?"

Mick stared at the two of them. Both looked serious. Both seemed to want him to stay.

"Jessie will show you what to do," Sandi said with a grin. "I'll see you later."

Jessie led him away from the house, into a field. They walked the length of it in silence, Jessie in front, Mick trailing behind, wondering what she thought about him, whether she hated him for what Sandi said his father had done.

She walked him to the far end of the field, and stopped beside a fence. On the other side of it was a paved road, its two lanes separated by concrete dividers. The road looked as if it hadn't seen any traffic or maintenance in years. Weeds had shouldered their way up through the asphalt in dozens of places, making it look like a crudely stitched quilt.

"That's where it happened, you know," Jessie said.

Mick looked at her. It. The accident. He looked from the road to Jessie. What was she going to do, rub his nose in it? Go ahead, he thought grimly. I can take it.

"If you go down that way, you end up at your grandfather's place," she went on. "They built a new road a couple of years later, over there." She gestured in the direction from which they had just come. "This one isn't used anymore. But it hap-

67

pened right there." She moved a little farther along the fence and pointed to a spot on the road that, to Mick, looked like any other spot. "My mother used to bring me out here when I was little," she said. "See that drainpipe over there?"

He nodded. The pipe came out at the edge of the wide gravelled shoulder right over the deep ditch that nudged up against the fence.

"My mother told me that pipe was red with my grandfather's blood. She said it stayed like that for a long time, that the rain never quite washed it away."

Mick stared at the pipe. He could imagine it coated with a dead man's blood. Then Jessie turned and looked him straight in the eye.

"Frankly," she said, "I find that pretty hard to believe. Blood just doesn't stick to metal like that, not in a good hard rain. But my mother tends to be pretty dramatic. I guess you can't blame her, though, seeing that it was her father."

She turned so that her back was to the road and she leaned against the fence, looking across the fields. "People around here say the Standishes are land-hungry," she said. "They say the Elliots up the way think they're better than everyone else. They say the apple never falls far from the tree."

*They* say? Who was *They*? And what about her? Mick wondered. What did she say?

"A lot of people in Haverstock will think things about you based purely on the fact that you're Dan Standish's son," she continued.

Mick peered into her green eyes. It took more

courage than he knew he had just to say two words. "And you?"

"Me?" She shrugged. "I'd rather make up my own mind. If I decide I don't like you, it'll be for a reason I discover all by myself, and not because someone tells me I shouldn't like you because of something your father did before you were even born. I never knew my grandfather, and I'm sorry about that. But it's not *your* fault. This — " She nodded at the place on the road where her grandfather had met his end. "This has nothing to do with you or me, okay?"

He nodded.

"Good," she said, and grinned. "Now, what do you know about using a hoe?"

"If she wants to see Mick, then I don't see any harm in it," Aunt Charlene was saying when Mick entered the kitchen.

"If who wants to see me?" he asked.

Aunt Charlene whirled around, her hands white with the flour with which she had just dusted the counter, getting ready to roll out pastry for yet another pie. Mick had never seen a person make as many pies as his aunt did. If he were judging the pie contest she was planning to enter, he'd award her first prize for her ginger-peach pie. He'd never tasted anything as sweet and juicy.

"Who wants to see me?" Mick repeated.

Uncle Jim shook his head, making it clear that Mick had just committed the crime of incredibly bad timing.

"Your grandmother," he said. "Your mother's mother. Edith Menzies."

His grandmother? Mick's mother had never told him her own mother was alive. Mick had always believed that his mother's parents were dead.

"She lives in the nursing home in town," Aunt Charlene said. "She's old, but she's still mentally alert."

"That may be overstating the case," Uncle Jim said.

Aunt Charlene gave him a sharp look. "She's heard you're in town, Mick, and she wants to see you. I'll run you down there after supper if you want."

It was strange to see someone as small as Aunt Charlene handling Uncle Jim's big old pickup so expertly. To look at her, you wouldn't have thought she knew the first thing about stick shifts and four-wheel drive. You sure wouldn't have figured she'd be able to manoeuvre a pickup in a tiny nursing home parking lot without breaking a sweat. While Mick watched her back into a space near the home's side door, he got the feeling that there might be other things about his aunt that he'd been wrong about, that maybe there was more to her than rolling pins, terry-cloth aprons, pie recipes, and dreams of a brand-new kitchen.

The nursing home was bright and clean, the staff smiling and seemingly pleased to meet him. A couple of the older ones knew Dan and politely inquired about him. Mick wondered how much of their courtesy was real, and how much was layered on for his benefit.

Aunt Charlene led him down a wide corridor to a bright sunroom where a dozen or more old people sat in front of a big-screen TV. From a distance, the scene seemed almost heart-warming — old people gathered together at the end of the day to enjoy some entertainment. But when Mick actually entered the room he noticed that the TV was turned up loud to compensate for hearing problems, and that some people weren't even looking at the screen, but were staring with unfocussed eyes at sights that were invisible to everyone else. Fully half were in wheelchairs. Mick was relieved when his grandmother turned out to be one of those who was actually watching the blaring game show.

Following Aunt Charlene's introduction, Edith Menzies glared up at Mick for a few moments, then struggled to her feet and shuffled out of the room. Confused by her lack of enthusiasm, Mick glanced at his aunt.

"I think she wants some privacy," Aunt Charlene shouted above the din of the TV. "Let's go to her room."

Mick nodded and followed the bent figure of his grandmother. She was already sitting in a rocking chair beside her bed when he and Aunt Charlene caught up with her.

"Well, you sure do look like your father," she said. It didn't sound like a compliment. "How is he, anyway?"

"Okay, I guess."

"Out of prison, is he?" Her face was as wrinkled as a prune, her watery eyes as sour as lemons. She had none of the sweet gentleness that Mick associated with his mother, or with grandmothers in general.

"He's out," Mick said.

"Come here."

Mick advanced cautiously.

"Sit down."

He perched stiffly on the edge of the bed.

"Tell me about your mother," she said, her voice softer now. "I never saw her again after she left here. She was angry with me, and to tell you the truth, the feeling was mutual. Was she a good mother?"

Aunt Charlene edged toward the door. "I'll leave you two alone," she said softly. "Take your time, Mick. I'll wait for you outside."

"Well?" Mick's grandmother said. "Aren't you going to answer me?"

"She was a good mother," Mick said. As good as a mother could be who hid the truth from her only son. "She must have been pretty mad at you not to have wanted to see you or talk to you for nine years." He couldn't help wondering: Were *you* a good mother?

The old woman shook her head slowly. "Lisa was stubborn," she said. "Stubborn and too proud to admit it when she was wrong." She peered at Mick, then said, "What about you? Are you wild and reckless like your father? Or are you stubborn and proud like your mother?" She didn't seem to expect an answer, and didn't pause for him to give one, but kept right on talking.

"It took a long time before your grandfather and I were blessed with a child. And what a smart thing she was, right from the start. Your mother was one of the brightest girls in her class all through school," she said. "By the time she was in her senior year, everyone was sure she'd be going away to university. She was offered several scholarships, you know. All she had to do was take her pick — which school did she want to go to? She had a nice boyfriend, too. And, no, it wasn't your father. She'd dated him on and off all through high school. One minute she'd be declaring that she loved Dan Standish, the next she'd be saying that he wasn't serious enough, he'd never settle down. Then she took up with that nice Les Culver. He'd just finished his police training and had been assigned here with the OPP. He's still here, you know."

"I met him," Mick said, thinking back to Sandi's kitchen.

"He's a good man. Dependable. When Lisa took up with him I thought, finally, someone who will make her happy, who'll look after her. Les would have encouraged her to continue her studies, and would have waited for her while she did. The two of them had such potential. She could have been anything she wanted. He could have worked his way up. I had such high hopes.

"Then she fell for Danny again. Head over heels, is how she described it. Head over heels, and pregnant. I remember the night she told me. I'm not

73

ashamed to admit that I was good and angry. Lisa could have been anything. She could have gone anywhere. She could have had any man she wanted. But she wanted Dan Standish, and the next thing anyone knew, she was talking about marrying him. She did, too, even after what happened. Got Mr. Engle, the United Church minister, to marry them right down there in the jail, if you can imagine. I have to stand by him, she told me. She refused to believe he'd done anything wrong. Les tried to reason with her. Danny was drunk, he told her, too drunk to have been driving. But she refused to hear a negative word about Dan, let alone the worst. And then when he went off to prison, she went with him to be close by — so he could see his child, was how she put it. We had a big fight before she left. I told her she was a fool to follow him, that she should think of herself and her child and never mind Dan Standish. She never spoke to me again after that. I used to write to her. She sent every letter back unopened."

"Did you ever send her money?" Mick asked.

His grandmother looked surprised. "Money? Me? Your grandfather left us with nothing but debts. I had to sell the farm after he died. I scraped by as best I could running the lunch counter at the five and dime, but I never had a nickel to spare. No, I didn't send her any money." She looked closely at Mick. "Now you tell me, did she raise you up right? Did she ever talk about me? Was it hard for her . . . at the end?" Her voice caught on the words, and her eyes filled with tears. Suddenly she started to sob.

Her shoulders heaved as she gasped out her grief. "I should have gone to her. I shouldn't have been as stubborn as she was. I should have swallowed my pride and got on the bus and gone to see her at least once."

Mick stared helplessly at the old woman for a moment. Then, awkwardly, because he didn't know what else to do, he put a hand on her shoulder. She looked up at him and managed a weak smile while she dabbed at her tears with a tissue.

That night Mick couldn't sleep. He thought about what Sandi had told him, and how different her story was from the one he'd heard from his mother. He thought about what his grandmother had said, and what his mother's life might have been like if she hadn't fallen for Dan Standish. But mostly he thought about the spot on the road that Jessie had shown him. Something was wrong, he realized. If it had happened where Jessie said, something was very wrong.

"Tell me again," he said to her the next day.

"Tell you what?"

"Tell me exactly what happened."

"Mick, I don't — "

"Better yet, show me." He grabbed her by the hand and led her, half walking, half running, back across Sandi's field to the abandoned road. He climbed the fence and turned to help her, but she'd already scrambled over it. "Show me," he repeated.

"Mick, if you'd just tell me — "

"I will. I promise I will. But first you have to tell

me what your mother told you. How did it happen? Where?"

She frowned, but slowly turned to orient herself.

"There's the drainpipe," she said, "where my mother said she saw the blood. My grandfather was there when he was hit by the car. According to my mother, he'd been walking along this side of the road — "

"The side where he was hit? He was walking over here?"

Jessie nodded. "He was coming from down there," she said, "and he was walking along this side of the road, on the shoulder here. I know it doesn't look like much now, but back then this was *the* main road. If you follow it far enough, you get to the border."

It was an odd-looking road, too, with the wide paved expanse between the two lanes, and the low concrete dividers running right down the middle.

"Looks like there used to be three lanes," Mick said.

"There were. Way back when this road was built, it was designed with one lane going east, one going west, and a third lane in the middle for passing in both directions."

Mick looked at the road again, and imagined what might happen if two cars travelling in opposite directions tried to pass at the same time.

"Sounds dangerous," he said.

"It was. My mother says there were a couple of head-on collisions every year. That's why those concrete dividers were put there. They closed down the middle lane and put the dividers in to make sure that no one used it."

"Were the dividers there fifteen years ago?"

Jessie nodded.

"So your grandfather was over here, walking in the same direction as traffic, is that right?" He hoped she'd disagree with him, that she'd say something like, Oh no, that would have been dangerous. My grandfather always walked facing traffic. He was over on the other side, on the side of the road your father was driving on.

But she didn't say that.

She said, "He was on this side. Mr. Potato Head wouldn't walk on the other side of the road."

"Mr. Potato Head?"

"My grandfather's bulldog. He liked to poke along this fence. The one on the other side is made of barbed wire."

Mick glanced across the asphalt and saw that she was right.

"That land belongs to someone else, a really old guy who used to keep his bull in that field. Apparently Mr. Potato Head got his nose caught on the barbed wire once, and after that he avoided that side of the road. He stuck to this side. And my grandfather stuck to Mr. Potato Head. But Mom says he always wore his reflector jacket when he was out walking, so that even if he couldn't see the cars, they could always see him."

"Reflector jacket?"

"An old jacket that he stuck reflector tape on, front and back. Mom still has it. It has a big X on the back and two big Xs on the front. Apparently people around here thought it was pretty funny. Mind you, the way my mother tells it, people around here thought it was pretty funny that my grandfather actually used to walk his dog."

Mick didn't understand what was so odd about that. He thought of all the people he saw every day, taking their pets out for a walk. If you had a dog, you walked it. Big deal.

"Wouldn't it have been strange if he *didn't* walk his dog?" he said.

Jessie smiled and shook her head. "This isn't the big city, Mick. Look around you. It's doggy heaven. You just turn them loose and let them run. Nobody around here wastes their time walking their dogs. Well, nobody except my grandfather. He'd be out here every morning at six, and every night at eleven, no matter what. My mom said he even used to go out in the dead of winter. He was out here one time in a blizzard, and stayed out for so long that my grandmother was terrified he'd frozen to death. Around here, that made him eccentric. People used to laugh about it and tease him."

Country people were strange, Mick decided. Or starved for genuinely funny things to laugh about. Or maybe it didn't matter where you were, maybe there were always a certain number of weird people around.

"Okay," he said, "so your grandfather and his dog were walking way over on this side of the road, and he was wearing reflectors, which means that anyone coming up behind him or toward him would have seen him. Right?"

Jessie nodded.

Mick swung around, facing town. "And Dan was coming from that direction." He pointed. "He was driving toward your grandfather and he was over there, on the opposite side of these concrete dividers. Right?"

Jessie nodded.

"Your grandfather was walking way over here on the shoulder. Right?"

Another nod.

"Which means he would have seen Dan coming, even if Dan didn't see him."

"Well, yeah. I guess so."

"And he would have noticed if Dan's car seemed out of control, if Dan seemed to be driving crazy."

Jessie nodded.

"He would have noticed and he would have reacted, right? Maybe he would have dived across that ditch, for instance."

Jessie's eyes narrowed.

"What are you saying, Mick?"

Mick pictured the scene: the old man with the reflector jacket, strolling down the road behind his bulldog. The old man gazing into the distance and seeing approaching headlights, maybe noticing that they were swerving a little more than they should have been, but probably feeling safe because he was on the other side of the concrete dividers. Or maybe he started edging toward the ditch beside the gravel shoulder. Maybe he tensed up, ready to leap across the ditch, out of the path of the meandering car. He was ready, but probably he was still thinking, I'm over here, on the safe side of the dividers. A car would likely be stopped, or at least deflected, by those dividers. I've got nothing to worry about. And then . . .

"Mick? What's the matter?"

He looked into Jessie's concerned eyes, but he couldn't make himself say the words. He couldn't force himself to say what he now believed to be true — that it wasn't an accident, not even a stupid, drunken one. It was murder. Cold-blooded murder.

# Chapter Six

Mick couldn't sleep. He kept thinking about Dan wrenching that steering wheel to the left, probably gunning the engine at the same time to make sure he got up and over the low concrete dividers. Wrenching the wheel and gunning the engine and running down another human being. He could almost hear the sickening thud and feel the car shudder as it hit Barry McGerrigle, sending him careening through the night air before finally crashing down to the gravel surface of the shoulder, his head bouncing off the sharp metal edge of the drainpipe. Bouncing, then lying limp. Dying, then dead. Dan wasn't some stupid drunk loser. He was a murderer. But that wasn't the worst of it.

The worst was his mother.

Mick felt sick to his stomach thinking about her because no matter how you looked at it, one of only two things had to be true where she was concerned. Either she had known all along that what Dan had done that night was no accident, in which case she had lied to Mick. Lied to him repeatedly. Your poor father, she'd said. It was an accident, she'd said. Your father doesn't deserve to be in prison. You have to believe me, Mick. You have to believe in your father. Promise me, Mick. Promise me.

Either she had been lying to him the whole time, or she'd been deceived like Mick. She'd believed Dan's story — Dan's lie. And because she'd believed it, because she thought it was all a mistake, she'd stood by him. She had followed him to the miserable little town near the prison instead of staying in Haverstock or going somewhere else and starting over. She'd even married him. She'd taken whatever jobs she could find, and those were mostly low-paying. Most of what she made she spent on lawyer's fees. She'd worked and worried about Dan, and the whole time she'd been deceived.

Those were the only two possibilities — that his mother had been duped, or that she'd been a lair. Either way, Mick felt betrayed. He ached with bitterness. He needed to know for sure which was true. It would be the first question he asked when Dan returned, and the last words he'd ever speak to him. There was no way, knowing what he now knew, that he could live with Dan any longer. He'd run away first. He'd go to the Davidsons or, if that wasn't possible, he'd run. Either way, once Mick knew the whole truth, Dan was a thing of the past.

"What are you talking about?" Jessie said when he told her. "Are you saying that your father killed my grandfather on purpose?"

Mick hadn't planned on telling her or anyone else. But the facts kept eating at him, like rust working on iron, until his resolve had sprung a leak and he found himself at the Stiles's farm, pulling Jessie down the driveway, well away from the screened porch where Mrs. Stiles sat, patching a pair of denim overalls.

"That would mean it was murder," Jessie said, "and that's just plain crazy."

"Why?" Mick said. "What's so crazy about it? Isn't that exactly what your mother's been saying for years?"

"Well, sure, but that's because it was her father."

"Maybe she's been saying it because it's true."

Jessie shook her head in disbelief. "Aren't you forgetting a few things?"

"Like?"

"Like the fact that your Uncle Jim was in the car with your father. If your father had run down my grandfather on purpose, don't you think your uncle would have noticed? Don't you think he would have told the police?"

"He might have," Mick said. He peered into Jessie's moss-green eyes, wondering if she thought he was insane. Wondering, too, how much more deranged she'd consider him when he finished telling her everything. "You have to promise you won't say a word to anyone about what I'm going to tell you. At least, not until I figure everything out."

Jessie's sunny face clouded. "You're not kidding

about this, are you? You really think your uncle lied to the police."

Mick nodded gravely.

"But why? Why would he do something like that?"

Mick had puzzled over that question for most of the night: Why would a nice responsible guy like Uncle Jim let his drunken brother get behind the wheel of a car? Why wouldn't he do everything in his power to wrestle the car keys from Dan?

"I think he was being blackmailed," Mick said. "Sandi saw them arguing about who was going to drive that night. She said Dan said something to Uncle Jim — she couldn't hear what it was — but right away they stopped fighting and Uncle Jim threw the keys at Dan. Why would he do that?"

"You tell me," Jessie said.

"Because Dan forced him to back down. Dan was blackmailing Uncle Jim." Briefly Mick outlined the conversation between Uncle Jim and Uncle Buddy that he had overheard in the barn.

Jessie looked sceptical. "And you think he also blackmailed your uncle into saying my grandfather's death was an accident, when it was really murder?"

Mick's stomach churned as violently as it had when the realization first dawned on him. "That's exactly what I think. I wish there was some way I could talk to someone who was involved with the trial. Someone who'd be able to tell me who said what, what kind of evidence was presented."

"Why don't you talk to your uncle?"

Mick shook his head. "If he lied to cover up a murder, that's serious. If I ask him about it, he'll either refuse to talk about it, or he'll do what he did fifteen years ago — he'll lie."

Jessie nodded. She considered the matter for a few moments. "Well, I guess the next best person to talk to would be Mr. Dietrich," she said.

"Who?"

"Arthur Dietrich. He was your father's lawyer. Next to your father, he's the person my mother dislikes the most — no offense. And next to your father and your uncle, he's the person who probably knows the most about what happened that night — or at least who said what about what happened."

"Do you know where I can find this Mr. Dietrich?"

"Sure," Jessie said. "He has an office over in Morrisville. I bet we could get a lift over there with Heck."

Mick made a face. Heck was such a sour old man.

"He's not as bad as you think," Jessie said with a laugh. "*And* he drives over to Morrisville every week to see his doctor."

Mick was surprised. "Don't you have a doctor here?"

"Of course we do," Jessie said. She sounded so insulted that Mick was sorry he'd asked. Then she shrugged. "Doctors we have. Heart specialists we don't have."

"Heck has heart problems?"

Jessie nodded. She checked her watch. "If we hurry, we can catch a ride with him today."

For the first couple of kilometres, Heck didn't say a word, and Mick began to think the trip would be painless. He peered out the window at gravel and fences and ditches and field after field of green, some of it pasture filled with grazing livestock, some of it planted with beans and corn, peas and squash, all bushing out above the soil in neat green lines. Jessie sat in the middle of the pickup's cab, staring straight ahead for the most part, pointing out the odd item of interest.

"Where do you want me to drop you once we get to Morrisville?" Heck asked suddenly.

Mick had no idea what to answer. He glanced at Jessie to catch her eye, to signal her somehow that he didn't want to reveal their destination to anyone, not even good old Heck. But she had already turned to Heck, so the best Mick could do was nudge her with his elbow.

"You can leave us at the plaza," she said. If she'd registered his nudge, she gave no indication of it.

"Going to the movies, are you?" Heck said.

"Yeah," Mick said eagerly. Good cover, he thought. And end of discussion on the subject.

"No, of course not," Jessie said. "Mick wanted to see a movie. But the only one playing this afternoon is for little kids. We're just going to wander around. Maybe we'll stop by the bookstore. A book's better than a movie any day — at least, that's what my father always used to say. Mick's quite a mystery buff, you know."

"Is that right?" Heck said.

And that was the end of all conversation until Heck pulled into the plaza parking lot.

"I won't be long," he told them. "If you want a lift back, be here at four."

Jessie flashed him a high-voltage grin. "Thanks, Heck," she said. "That's really sweet of you."

Mick almost fell over when the old man actually blushed.

"See?" Jessie said after the battered truck pulled away. "I told you he wasn't so bad."

"Are you kidding?" Mick said. "That smile of yours would probably turn Dracula, the Wolfman and Frankenstein's monster into little blobs of putty."

"I'll take that as a compliment," Jessie said, and turned the smile on him.

Arthur Dietrich's office was located in an old-fashioned stone house with gingerbread trim and a white wooden veranda that ran around three sides. The enamelled sign beside the front door read: A. Dietrich, Wills and Estate Planning.

Mick looked at the sign, then at Jessie. "You sure this is the right guy?"

"Positive," Jessie said. "His daughter's on the basketball team with me. He comes to all the games." She pushed open the screen door. Mick followed her into the cool but sunny interior, where a middle-aged woman sat at a desk, tapping away on a keyboard.

"We'd like to see Mr. Dietrich," Jessie said.

The woman examined them coolly. "And do you have an appointment?"

Jessie shook her head. "I'm Jessie Stiles," she said, "and this is Mick Standish, Dan Standish's son. I'm sure if you tell Mr. Dietrich we're here, he'll want to see us."

The woman behind the desk looked anything but sure of this. She waved Jessie and Mick into a pair of chairs in the reception area, then picked up the phone and spoke quietly into it. A look of surprise flashed in her eyes when the door marked PRIVATE flew open, and a tall balding man strode past her, right over to Jessie and Mick.

"Jessie, good to see you again," he said, but his eyes were already on Mick, appraising him. "Good Lord, you're the image of your father. I've never seen such a strong resemblance." He thrust a hand at Mick. "Arthur Dietrich," he said. "Pleased to make your acquaintance, Mick. What can I do for you two?"

"We'd like to speak to you about Mick's father's case," Jessie said.

Mr. Dietrich looked surprised, but nodded all the same. "Of course," he said. "Come in. Come in." He led them back to his office.

"But Mr. Dietrich, you have an appointment with Mr. Rollins in ten minutes," the secretary reminded him.

"Well, why don't you call him and ask him if he can come in a little later? He won't mind. He's probably sleeping behind his desk even as we speak. Bob Rollins manages the real-estate office across the street," Mr. Dietrich explained to Jessie and Mick. "He wakes up just long enough to re-calculate the interest on his investments — and to wander across the street to see if he can get some tax advice from me, free of charge, of course. He's also my brother-in-law."

He shut the door behind them and waited until they had claimed a pair of comfortable leather chairs before he sank down into the big padded swivel chair behind his desk.

"So, Mick, what is it you want to know?"

"You were my father's lawyer, right?"

"That's right," Mr. Dietrich said. "I was."

"Then I'd like to know whatever you can tell me about my father's case."

Mr. Dietrich frowned and glanced at Jessie, who nodded. "How much do you know?" he asked.

"Not much," Mick admitted. He felt like a complete fool. *Yes, sir, my father was in prison for nine years. But no, sir, I have no idea how that happened. I know absolutely nothing. Apparently no one felt that this was information I needed . . .* "I know that Jessie's grandfather was killed," Mick said. "And I know my father went to prison for it. But that's about it. I was hoping you'd be able to fill me in on the details of the case. That is, unless it's confidential or something."

"There's nothing confidential about it. It's a matter of public record," Mr. Dietrich said. He sighed and leaned back in his chair. "It seems like such a long time ago. Let me see, I'd been in town for about two years — I settled here fresh out of law school — when I got a call from your grandfather asking me to go down to the jail to see about your father. At the time, I had a general practice — property transfers, contracts, wills, that sort of thing. I was doing pretty well, too, because there was only one other lawyer in the area besides me, and he was getting on in age. I'd handled a bit of work for your grandfather — contracts with the canneries and so forth. In fact, I was in the middle of some work for your grandmother at the time Dan was arrested."

Mick frowned. Something didn't sound right. "Aren't you a criminal lawyer?"

"No, never was. Your father's trial would have been my first."

"I don't understand," Mick said. "My father had been accused of a serious crime. Why didn't my grandfather hire a lawyer with criminal experience?"

"That's exactly what I wondered," Mr. Dietrich said. "As a matter of fact, I refused the case at first and strongly urged your grandfather to call someone who had handled cases like your father's before. But he wouldn't hear of it. 'You know my family, Art,' he said to me, 'and we know you.' He seemed to think that was pretty important — that we knew each other, and that he trusted me.

"Your grandfather told me that your father had been involved in some kind of accident, and that a man had been killed. He wanted me to go over to the jail and see what I could do. So I did. When I got there, your father was in pretty rough shape.

He'd been drinking, and he looked pretty confused. When I questioned him, he told me he didn't remember a thing. He admitted that he'd had a few beers. He recalled picking a fight with Barry McGerrigle down at the hotel. He also remembered Jim showing up and arguing with him about who was going to drive home. But he said he didn't remember anything after that until he woke up on the side of the road with the lights of a police car flashing in his face and Jim saying, 'Look what you've done now, Danny boy.' He seemed more than a little surprised to find himself sitting in jail."

Mick nodded. This was something interesting, something that might lead somewhere. "What did my Uncle Jim mean, Look what you've done?"

Mr. Dietrich shrugged. "I suppose he was referring to the consequences of drinking and driving," he said. "Anyway, the most I could get out of your father the first time I spoke to him was that he didn't remember what happened. I assumed he would plead innocent to the charge that had been laid. I told him I'd be back to see him later, after he'd had a little rest.

"When I went back to the jail that afternoon, your father was telling a different story. He said that the whole thing had come back to him. If you want my opinion, though, it was Jim who reminded him, because it was apparently shortly after Jim paid him a visit that your father's memory 're-turned.' Now the story he told was that he was driving, perhaps a little erratically on account of the drink, and all of a sudden someone appeared on the road out of nowhere and before your father could swerve to avoid him, he'd hit him."

But first, Mick knew, he'd jumped a concrete divider and crossed a lane. The swerving was the cause of the death, not an attempt to prevent it.

"After Dan told me what he'd remembered, he asked me if the charge would be manslaughter."

"Why manslaughter?" Mick said. Sandi had told him that was the charge. "Why not murder?"

"There was no intent to cause death or bodily harm," Mr. Dietrich said. "This was a case of culpable homicide due to criminal negligence."

"Huh?"

"Your father shouldn't have been driving when he was as drunk as he was," Mr. Dietrich explained. "Your father didn't put up any fight. He said if the charge was manslaughter, he'd be prepared to plead guilty."

"What?" Mick couldn't believe his ears. "He actually pleaded *guilty*?"

Mr. Dietrich nodded.

Mick slumped in his chair. One of his questions had just been answered — but Mick would have been just as happy not to have known this particular bit of truth. The whole time that Mick's mother had been comparing Dan to Hurricane Carter and Donald Marshall, Dan Standish had not only *not* been wrongly convicted — he'd actually pleaded guilty. It was a smart move, Mick thought grimly, to plead guilty to a charge of manslaughter when you'd just committed cold-blooded murder.

"Dan said he supposed pleading guilty was the

right thing to do. The main thing that seemed to worry him was what the sentence would be." I'll bet, Mick thought. "He and your mother weren't married yet, but . . . " He blushed. "He was concerned about her having to cope alone, with a child on the way. I told him I couldn't predict what the sentence might be. A lot depended on the circumstances and on the particular judge who would hear his plea. I told him he could end up with anywhere from a few months to fifteen or twenty years. He wanted to know how likely he was to get sentenced at the lighter end of the spectrum. When I said I couldn't guarantee anything, he said he supposed it didn't matter, he'd have to plead to it anyway. I think he might have been counting on getting a fairly light sentence. He might have, too, if Delbert Johnson had heard the case."

"Who's Delbert Johnson?"

"*Judge* Delbert Johnson. Born and raised in Haverstock. A great pal of your grandfather's, Mick. Knew the boys, too. Knew your father pretty well. I think Dan was hoping that would help. But Del excused himself from the case — said he felt he couldn't be impartial. A judge from outside the district was called in. He turned out to be a law-and-order man, the kind who believes in good stiff sentences that will set an example to the public at large. When Dan got up to make his plea, that judge threw the book at him. Gave him ten years.

"Still, you have to give Dan some credit for the way he handled himself. He stood up like a man and accepted full responsibility for his actions."

Not full responsibility, Mick thought. Not even close.

"He was prepared to pay for what he had done, which I thought showed great maturity. He was only twenty years old at the time, and he didn't try to weasel out of the matter. He didn't blame anyone else for what had happened. In fact, if it hadn't been for your grandmother, I might have remembered the whole affair differently. It might have been an inspiration to me to see a young man do the right thing."

"What do you mean? What did my grandmother have to do with this?"

"She was devastated by what happened. She was ailing at the time — she had cancer and had been waging a tough struggle against it. At the same time, she'd been making her plans. In fact, the main reason I'd got to know your family as well as I did was that your grandmother wanted a will drawn up. Her clergyman had recommended me. I met with her a couple of times to discuss the matter. She wanted to leave a piece of property — her father's property — to Dan. She had me draw up the papers in secret, and made me swear not to tell anyone in the family. Apparently your grandfather was opposed to Dan getting that land, so she had me draw up the will for her and swear that it wouldn't come to light until after she was gone. When Dan pleaded guilty to the death of Barry McGerrigle, it really tore her up. She was completely devastated. She called me in and had me change her will. Had me cut Dan out completely. About a month after he went to prison, her health failed. She didn't live out the year. Things were never the same in your family after that — not with your grandmother gone and Dan in prison. And that's just about all I know about the matter."

"What about my Uncle Jim?" Mick asked.

"What about him?"

"Did you ever talk to him about what happened that night?"

Mr. Dietrich shook his head. "There wasn't any need to."

"Why wasn't he charged, too?" Jessie asked. "He *let* Dan drive. Isn't that also negligent?"

"Jim jumped into the car at the last minute to try to stop Dan," Mr. Dietrich said. "He was trying to prevent a disaster."

"Too bad he didn't," Mick murmured. He stood up and thanked the lawyer for his time. At least one question had been answered, maybe the most important one. But a few more had been raised, each as puzzling and disturbing as the original one.

As Jessie and Mick walked down Mr. Dietrich's veranda steps, Heck Dinsmore's pickup truck slid by, and Mick was sure that Heck looked in their direction and saw them. But when he met them at the plaza as arranged, all that Heck said was, "So, did you uncover any good mysteries?"

Mick looked down at his empty hands while Jessie said, "No, we couldn't find anything that Mick hadn't already read."

"Right," said Heck. "Pile in now and let's get going."

# Chapter Seven

Heck dropped them at Jessie's place. Standing at the end of the Stiles's lane next to the mailbox anchored in a concrete-filled milk can, Mick looked toward the big square clapboard house and saw Mrs. Stiles on the porch, exactly where they had left her. She was looking right at them, watching her daughter talking to the son of a murderer. Watching and, Mick guessed, hating.

Jessie saw where Mick was looking and glanced back at the house. There was no trace of a smile on her face as she raised a hand and waved to her mother.

"Don't worry about her," Jessie said. "She may have sharp eyes, but even she can't hear us way out here." She perched on the top rail of the fence that separated Stiles property from the wild grass growing in the ditch. "So, what do you think about what Mr. Dietrich said?"

"Not good." A gross understatement, like calling a hurricane a little wind, or an earthquake a small shake-up.

"Mr. Dietrich said your dad couldn't remember at first what had happened. He said he thought he was going to plead innocent, but then he suddenly changed his mind and pleaded guilty. Does that make any sense to you? Wouldn't it have made more sense for him to stick to his original plan to plead innocent?"

Mick had thought about that all the way back from Morrisville, and had come up with what he thought was the only logical explanation. But before he told Jessie what he had concluded, he wanted to put his theory to the test.

"I think it's time I talked to my uncle," he said. "I know Dan was blackmailing him, but I can't believe Uncle Jim would let him get away with murder. He doesn't seem like that kind of guy. I want to know exactly what went on between the first and second times Mr. Dietrich talked to Dan." He wasn't looking forward to confronting his uncle, but he couldn't see any way around it.

Jessie reached out and touched his shoulder. "Nervous, huh?" she said, and offered him a smile.

He hated to admit it. "Yeah. A little."

He tried the house first, but found only Aunt Charlene, standing at an ironing board, working her way through a small stack of laundry.

"Have you seen Uncle Jim?" Mick asked.

"I think he's in the barn." She looked cautiously at him. "I hope you don't mind, Mick, but I put a lot of your things in the wash."

Mick felt his cheeks redden. She was his aunt, but

he barely knew her. And yet she'd gathered up his dirty clothes — *all* of his dirty clothes — and . . .

"I would have asked you first," she said quickly, "but you're hardly ever here."

"It's okay," Mick said. He should really be thanking her, not making her feel bad. "Really, it's no problem."

She nodded and turned her attention back to her ironing.

"Aunt Charlene?" He hesitated. How could he put the question he wanted to ask? How could he pose it without alerting her to trouble? "Did you know my father well?"

She considered this a moment. "Well, yes, I guess so."

"What was he like?"

The question seemed to take her by surprise. "Well," she said with a little shrug, "you know."

Mick shook his head. "No, I don't, not really. That's what I'm trying to figure out — what kind of guy would do what he did, and why my mother stood by him all those years. Why she — " He stopped. He'd been going to say, why she made me promise to be loyal to him, too, but he suddenly decided against it. "What did *you* think of my father?"

Aunt Charlene finished ironing a blouse. She put it on a hanger and hooked the hanger over the top of the kitchen door. As she lifted a tablecloth from the laundry basket, she said, "I guess you could say he was a little wild. He was so much younger than Jim and Buddy. Everyone said your grandmother spoiled him. He didn't have as many chores as the older boys. And he could charm your grandmother out of almost any punishment." She ran the hot iron over the checkered cloth.

"Was he bad?" Mick asked.

Aunt Charlene blinked in surprise. "Bad? What do you mean?"

"My whole life he's been in and out of prison. Was he always like that? Was he always such a loser?"

"Mick!" She was so surprised that her hand stopped moving. Mick didn't know a lot about ironing — he hadn't done much of it — but he did know that if you didn't keep the iron moving, you could burn the material.

"Uh, Aunt Charlene." He nodded at the cloth on the ironing board.

Aunt Charlene looked down at it.

"Oh!" she cried, and lifted the iron. Her face relaxed. "No harm done." She resumed her ironing, but her breathing was quick, and Mick knew that she was upset about something. He waited. "Your father wasn't bad," she said at last, her voice low, almost a whisper.

"Wasn't bad?" Mick said. "Just killed a guy, is all. I've been thinking about that a lot, since I've been here. I've been thinking about that and you know what? I think I'd give anything to know exactly what was going through his head that night, exactly what made him do what he did."

Aunt Charlene's hands gripped the handle of the iron tighter as she finished the edges of the table-cloth.

"What's done is done, Mick, and there's no changing it," she said slowly. "I know that, from your perspective, it must all seem pretty terrible. But I guess he's paid for what happened. Maybe it's best just to set it all aside now."

"It's best to set all *what* aside now?" boomed a voice from the back door.

Aunt Charlene was so startled her feet almost left the floor. "Jim, you scared me to death."

Uncle Jim kicked off his big barn boots and padded across the kitchen in his sock feet. He got a pitcher of lemonade out of the fridge, and pulled a couple of glasses from the cupboard. "Can I pour you one, Mick?"

Mick nodded.

Uncle Jim set a glass of icy lemonade in front of him, set another on the counter for Aunt Charlene, then sank down onto one of the kitchen chairs. "So," he said, "you're quizzing your aunt about your old man, huh? Don't you know what they say, Mick?"

What Mick knew was that he hated it when people said that. They always thought they were being so clever, and they always made you answer — no, I *don't* know what they say — before they'd continue. Mick shook his head.

"If you want to know the whole story, you have to go straight to the horse's mouth. I grew up with your father. If there's something you want to know about him, ask me. I don't think there's anything I *don't* know."

Aunt Charlene turned off the iron, gathered up

all the finished work, and scurried out of the kitchen.

"So," Uncle Jim said, "what is it you want to know?"

Mick met his uncle's frank gaze. Uncle Jim, he realized, was not the kind of man who'd get himself good and drunk and cry for a month if anything ever happened to Aunt Charlene. Uncle Jim had probably never shed a tear in his life. He looked as hard as a fence post and as cool as the milk in the tanks out in the milk house.

"I want to know exactly what happened that night," Mick said.

Uncle Jim looked at him and laughed. "What do you want to dig all that up for? What's done is done. Your father's paid for what happened. Your mother paid, too, in her own way. What's the point of going back over that ground when there isn't a thing you can do to change it?"

"Who says I want to change it?" Mick said. "There's more than one reason to want to know the worst about a person."

Uncle Jim's eyes narrowed. He appraised Mick as if he were assessing a calf he was considering buying.

"You've got something on your mind, Mick," he said. "You want to tell me what it is?"

Mick studied his uncle a moment.

"Trade you," he said at last. "I'll tell you if you tell me."

A grin cut across Uncle Jim's wind weathered face. "You're a real dealer, aren't you? Okay. We'll trade."

Mick drew in a deep breath. "The last time Dan was inside, I got lucky," he said. "I got myself some really great foster parents. He's an architect. Really successful. His wife reminds me of Mom. They told me if things didn't work out, they'd fix it so I could go back and live with them."

"And now you're planning how to make that happen, is that it?" Uncle Jim said. "Dig deep enough into Danny's life and maybe you'll hit pay dirt, something you can use to needle Danny until he takes a swing at you, something like that? That would just about do it, wouldn't it? You pick up the phone, make a call to the child welfare people, and you're back with the architect and his missus, is that it?"

Mick said nothing. He wasn't even surprised by how quickly his uncle had accepted his explanation. Uncle Jim thought so little of his own brother — who wouldn't, after what he had done? — that it wasn't much of a leap for him to believe that all Mick wanted was to cut free of Dan once and for all. Which he did. But first he had to know the truth: what had really happened, what lies he had been told all these years, and why. No one was going to hide anything from him anymore, and no one was going to stop him from digging out the whole story.

"What did your mother tell you?"

"She said it was an accident."

Uncle Jim shook his head. "I'm sure that's what she thought. But the only accident was that Danny didn't do something that stupid way before then."

"Are you going to tell me what happened?"

"If you're sure you want to know. You know what they say — if you don't want to know the answer, don't ask the question."

"I said I wanted to know, didn't I?"

"Okay." Uncle Jim finished his lemonade, then leaned well back in his chair. "Danny could really get under people's skin. He was the kind of guy who never showed up on time, always took the easy way out, never did a lick more work than he felt like doing. He had no trouble getting away with that on Standish land when our mother was alive. She was blind where Danny was concerned. Wouldn't hear a word of criticism about him. He's young, she'd say. Give him time, he'll learn, he'll settle down.

"Well, that summer Danny decided he didn't want to help out on Buddy's place anymore, or on mine, either, for that matter. We didn't pay him enough. What a joke, he got room and board, and an allowance from Mother, and he didn't want to do a lick of work in return. Anyway, he took a job with Barry McGerrigle. Why Barry was foolish enough to hire him, I'll never know. Danny's laziness wasn't exactly the best kept secret in town.

"Danny went to work for Barry, and right away there was trouble. Barry rode him pretty hard, but Danny put up with it because of what Barry had said he'd pay him — which sounded pretty high, if you want my opinion. Sounded like old Barry had Danny all figured out: put a carrot in front of him and watch him run. Then, at the end of the summer, Dan got his nose all out of joint because Barry

103

didn't pay him what he'd promised. He short-changed Dan. At least, that's what Dan claimed. Barry had a different point of view. He said he'd paid Danny *more* than he was worth.

"The night of the accident Dan was down at the hotel drinking — nothing new there. Heck Dinsmore was there, too, the old bum. All he cared about was drinking and making trouble. He'd rather do that than look after his wife and baby daughter. He was part of the whole mess, you know. He egged Danny on that night. Told him he agreed that Barry was a cheat and a liar and that Danny ought to do something about it. Anyway, Danny and Barry got into some kind of scuffle, and I was called to come down and get Dan. When I got there, Barry had already gone home. Dan had had too much to drink and he was in a rotten mood. He insisted on driving. We had a real wrangle over the car keys. Dan even took a swing at me. He made me so angry I threw the keys at him — " He paused and looked sombrely at Mick. "That's something I'll regret to my dying day," he said, shaking his head.

"I managed to get in the car before he pulled away. I figured if he did anything stupid, I'd grab the wheel from him. We started for home. Dan was driving okay — not great, but okay. I didn't feel like my life was at stake or anything. Then we came up the road by Barry McGerrigle's house, and what did we see but old Barry out there on the side of the road with his dog, just like he was every night at that time. Or maybe he was trying to cool down after the fight. Anyway, like I said, Danny wasn't

104

driving too straight and he hit Barry and killed him. That's it. End of story."

Mick sat in silent disappointment. He had, he realized, been expecting something more from his uncle. Instead, he got the same old cover-up. If he wanted the whole truth, it was clear he was going to have to dig for it.

"I know he had something on you, Uncle Jim," he said quietly.

Uncle Jim's face sharpened into a question. "What did you say?"

"I know he was blackmail— "

Uncle Jim's ham of a hand closed on Mick's mouth. He got up and strode into the back porch, nodding for Mick to follow him. He closed the door behind them, so that they were alone in the porch, so no one could hear them.

"You want to be careful what you say," Uncle Jim said, his voice a low rumble. "This is my home. I have to live here."

"I heard you," Mick said. His knees were shaking. He realized that he was afraid of his uncle. "I heard you and Buddy out in the barn talking about what Dan had on you. That's why you let him drive that night, isn't it? He was drunk and angry and acting like a jerk and he threatened to spill the beans if you didn't back off, didn't he?"

Uncle Jim said nothing.

"Why didn't you let him drive on his own? Why did you get in the car with him? You could have let him go out there and do what he did. You could have made him face up to it all by himself, without you to make excuses for him."

A dark frown creased Uncle Jim's weathered forehead. "I don't think you have a strong hold on the facts, Mick."

"Why did you get in the car with him? Why didn't you just let him hang himself?"

Uncle Jim studied him for a few moments, and as he did, Mick felt his cheeks start to burn. Uncle Jim was probably wondering what kind of son asked questions like that, what kind of son wished his father had been left alone to deal with the biggest mess of his life?

"He was pretty drunk, Mick," he said as last. "I thought if I didn't go with him, he'd hurt himself."

"But he didn't care about you. He would have hurt you if you'd given him the chance. Why did you care about what happened to him?"

"Mick — "

"You lied for him, didn't you? After he killed Barry McGerrigle, he blackmailed you into lying for him. What I don't understand is why he pleaded guilty. Why didn't he go all the way and plead innocent? Why didn't he try to use you to convince a jury to let him off? That would have been possible, wouldn't it? You could have said he lost control of the car, that he wasn't all that drunk."

Uncle Jim blinked in confusion. "Mick, I really don't — "

"You know what I'm talking about, Uncle Jim. I know he did it on purpose and that somehow he convinced you to help him cover it up. What I don't understand is why he pleaded guilty. If he had that much power over you, why didn't he get you to roll over completely? So are you going to tell me, or do you want me to go and ask Aunt Charlene for her opinion?"

Uncle Jim's face turned scarlet. He loomed over Mick, arm raised, and Mick braced himself for a blow. Then, suddenly, his uncle turned away and sank down onto an old wooden bench that ran under the porch's rear window. He buried his head in his hands. Mick wondered what he was thinking, what he was doing. When Uncle Jim finally raised his head again, his face was grey and grave.

"What I'm going to tell you, Mick, I never told another living soul. I'm only telling you because you seem to want to know badly enough to hurt innocent people to find out."

Mick smarted under the remark. He had threatened his uncle with blackmail. He had shown himself to be no better than Dan.

"I'll tell you, but first I want you to give me your word that you'll keep this strictly between the two of us. I can't enforce that, of course. I don't have any leverage. But if you give me your word, I'll trust you."

He extended a hand to Mick. Mick took it and they shook.

"Danny saw Barry on the side of the road, and before I could do a thing, he swerved the car toward him. Hit him straight on, killed him almost instantly. I guess I'm lucky I didn't end up in jail, too, for letting him drive in the first place."

"So it *was* murder," Mick said in a barely audible voice.

Uncle Jim nodded.

"And you let him get away with it."

"I'm not proud of what I did, Mick. And I want you to know I didn't just do it because Dan was blackmailing me. We fought about it — boy, did we fight about it. He threatened me, of course. And, yeah, I was afraid, because if Charlene had found out, she'd have left me, and I'd have lost more than a wife. I'd have lost this place, too. She owned half of it. We couldn't have got as far as we did without her salary paying the mortgage. And then there was your grandmother. She was sick at the time, and it would have killed her if she thought Dan had killed old Barry on purpose. As it was, the whole thing wore her down. She died three months after Danny went to prison.

"Still, though, I wasn't prepared to let him just walk out of there after what he did. I was in the car with him, Mick. I saw what happened. I saw what he did. I told him, you plead guilty to manslaughter and do your time like a man, and I'll keep the rest under my hat. I told him, you try to come out of this smelling like roses, and I don't care what happens to me, you'll go down for murder. I'm not an evil man, Mick. I know the difference between right and wrong. As it is, he served about as much time for manslaughter as he would have for second-degree murder."

"But it *was* murder?" Mick said. "It really was murder?"

Uncle Jim nodded.

Mick's knees buckled. He sank down onto the

bench next to his uncle. Suspecting was one thing, knowing was another. And knowing felt a whole lot worse than suspecting.

# Chapter Eight

The moon, full and high, cast a silvery sheen over the pastures that stretched from the back of Uncle Jim's house down to a winding river that formed the southern boundary of Standish land. Mick sat in the window of his cousin Lucy's bedroom and gazed out over the expanse of land. It was so wide, so open, with none of the cramped spaces and sharp corners that made up his familiar city landscape. He breathed in the fragrance of fresh-cut clover and grass, and tried to imagine Dan and his mother inhaling the same pure scent two decades before.

From the old metal chocolate box in his lap, he plucked the little black bottle that had once held his mother's perfume and, for the first time in a long time, unscrewed the cap. He held the bottle to his nose and breathed in deeply. Nothing. No scent remained, nothing to give that whiff of reality to the memory of his mother. Disappointed, he let the bottle fall from his hand.

He fingered the small bundle of letters in the bottom of the box, and pulled from it the three mystery envelopes addressed in strong straight black printing. His grandmother said she hadn't sent them. He was almost sure they hadn't been sent by Big Bill. Who then? Uncle Buddy? Uncle Jim? He let the envelopes fall back into the box. Did it even matter anymore? Everything he'd ever heard about his father had turned out to be a lie. His mother had lied about Dan's innocence. Dan had lied when he pleaded guilty to manslaughter instead of murder. Jim had lied — well, had failed to tell the truth — when he stood by silently and allowed Dan to answer to a crime less serious than the one he had committed. What did it matter, then, who had sent those fifty-dollar money orders to Mick's mother? What did any of it matter?

The next morning Mick took refuge on the back of a hay wagon out behind the barn. He hadn't slept much — couldn't — and he didn't feel like being around people. Being alone out in the country should have been easy, he thought. It wasn't. He hadn't been there more than twenty minutes when Uncle Jim appeared.

"You missed your breakfast," he said as he dropped down beside Mick on the wagon. "That's got your aunt worried. She thinks a man who passes on breakfast must be on death's doorstep."

Mick wished Uncle Jim would go away. He didn't want to talk to him, not about Dan, not about anything.

Uncle Jim sighed and laid a hand on Mick's

shoulder. "Look," he said, "about yesterday. You were the one who wanted to know, remember? You were the one asking all the questions."

"I know," Mick said.

"Okay," Uncle Jim said. "Just so we're straight on that." His hand fell from Mick's shoulder. "I have a job that needs doing. Something that'll maybe take your mind off your problems. Big Bill just took delivery on some firewood — "

"Firewood?" Mick said. "What for? Doesn't he have regular heating?"

"It's not for heating," Uncle Jim said. "It's for his fireplace. Big Bill loves a fire on a cold winter night. Always did."

"This isn't winter," Mick said. "Why's he buying firewood in the middle of the summer?"

"First of all, he isn't buying. Second, old Andy Lovering, across the way — " he nodded in the direction of the river " — had a tree come down in the last big storm. It's more firewood than he can store, so he gave some to Big Bill. His boy Arch dumped it in Big Bill's driveway first thing this morning. Someone has to pile it up in the shed. You think you can manage that?"

Mick shrugged. "Sure." Maybe Uncle Jim was right — it would give him something to do, without anyone bothering him.

Mick dragged an old wheelbarrow out from the crawl space under Big Bill's back porch. He wheeled it around to the driveway, filled it with firewood, and trundled it back to the shed where he emptied it piece by piece, building the base of what promised to be a wall of wood that would keep Big Bill's fireplace flaming for the rest of the winters of his life. Back and forth he went, loading, unloading, feeling his muscles stretch and pull with each load. The work was quiet, oddly comforting, almost therapeutic. It was a pleasure to give himself over to the physicality of the task, and satisfying to transform the chaos of the dumped wood into an orderly and substantial shape.

When he came around the side of the house to load the wheelbarrow for the fourth time, Big Bill was sitting out on the front steps, holding a mug of coffee in his big-knuckled hands.

"Being your father's son doesn't seemed to have spoiled you for an honest morning's work," he said, and cackled, as if he'd told a clever joke.

Mick worked with his back to the old man. He wondered if Big Bill knew what Uncle Jim knew, whether it was the truth of what had happened that night that was sticking in his throat, making him as bitter as a bucket of vinegar.

"I hear you were over in Morrisville the other day," Big Bill said. "Heard you met Art Dietrich."

Mick finished filling the wheelbarrow, then turned to look at his grandfather. How did he know where Mick had gone and who he had seen?

"A good man, that Dietrich," Big Bill said. "The kind of fellow who believes any job worth doing is worth doing well, so that it doesn't have to be done all over again."

Mick looked at the jumble of wood that covered

the driveway and wondered if this comment was a veiled criticism of the work he was doing.

"Your grandmother liked Dietrich," Big Bill said. "Liked him so much she trusted him with things she wouldn't tell members of her own family."

There was nothing complimentary in his tone now. Mick pushed the wheelbarrow past him, thinking the old man would stop talking if his audience walked away.

But he didn't. He got up, still holding his mug of coffee, and trailed behind Mick, talking the whole time. "She had Dietrich draw up her will. Did it behind my back. Had him come up to the house when I was out in the field. Brought him in, whispered her secrets in his ear, had him put it in that fancy legal lingo of his that her father's land was to go to Danny when she died. To Danny — " he spat the name " — who never did an honest day's work in his life."

Mick focussed every scrap of his attention on stacking the wood, wedging the smaller pieces into the spaces between the larger ones. He didn't want to hear anymore about Dan. He didn't even want to think about him. He emptied the wheelbarrow, and headed back for another load. Big Bill stuck with him.

"I'll bet Dietrich thought when he drew up that will the first time that he had himself a work of art that would stand forever. But I guess the joke was on him. After what happened, after Margaret saw what kind of man she'd left her father's land to, she had me telephone him. I didn't know why she wanted to see him, of course. And I'd been thinking I was in for a big fight with her about the will. I'd been racking my brain trying to figure out how to raise the subject. But in the end, I didn't have to do a thing. Margaret brought him back to the house and right there in front of him she tore up his piece of work, ripped that heavy fancy paper he used into little bitty pieces, and she said to him, 'Now then, Arthur, I think we need to start all over again.' She was real dignified about it. She spent a lifetime not wanting to hear the truth about Danny, but once she did hear it, she accepted it and she did the right thing."

Mick clutched a heavy wedge of firewood in each hand. It would have been easy — so easy — to whirl around and pound one or both of those wedges into his grandfather's head. Maybe then he'd shut up about Dan. Maybe everyone would stop talking about the whole mess. Mick drew in a deep breath. Then another. He drank the air in huge gulps, as if it contained a painkiller or a tranquilizer. Then, his hands shaking, he filled the wheelbarrow again and, while his grandfather rattled on, counted in his head to a hundred, to two hundred, to a thousand, until finally the job was done and Big Bill had gone back into his house.

Mick slid out of the front seat of the pickup and waved thanks and goodbye.

"Are you sure you don't want a lift home?" Aunt Charlene said. "I can pick you up on my way back."

"Thanks," Mick said, "but it's okay. I'm going out to Sandi's later. I'll be fine."

"Well, okay," Aunt Charlene said, sounding anything but okay, the reservation in her voice making him feel all of six years old instead of nearly sixteen. "You won't forget to go to the post office for me, will you?"

"I'm going there first," Mick assured her, "before I do anything else. Don't worry. I'll mail it."

"It" was Aunt Charlene's entry in the pie contest. Mick wondered if mailing the entry would mean an end to the stream of scrumptious creations she had been turning out since his arrival. If so, he'd be sorry. He had turned into a serious pie fan.

As he headed down the sidewalk to the post office — which wasn't a separate building, but a wicket next to the cash register in the drugstore — Mick held the envelope containing his aunt's recipe to the light. Was she entering her apple-cinnamon crumble, he wondered, or her deep dish blueberry?

*Umph.*

He collided with something — someone. Heck Dinsmore. A small sheaf of envelopes fluttered to the sidewalk as Heck reeled backward.

"Sorry," Mick said. He ducked automatically to scoop up the envelopes Heck had dropped, then froze. Still half-crouched, he stared up at the old man.

Heck's gnarled hand grabbed the envelopes from Mick.

"You should watch where you're going," he snapped, before turning to walk away.

Mick struggled to a standing position. He hurried after Heck and grabbed his arm.

Heck glowered at him. "What the devil is wrong with you, boy? First you bowl me over trying to get to the wicket before me. Now you're hanging onto me like a baby clinging to its mama."

"You're the one," Mick said, his throat clogged with surprise, his voice hoarse.

"The one? What are you talking about, the one?"

"You're the one who sent that money to my mother."

Heck shook his head impatiently. "You'd better get yourself a hat, boy. You've been out in the sun too long. I think you've fried your brain."

"I know it was you," Mick said. "I recognize that handwriting. I have a couple of your envelopes back at the house. I saved them. We could compare them. But I know it was you."

Heck tried to step around Mick, but Mick blocked his way.

"The only question is why," he said. "They came as regular as clockwork, Heck. Fifty dollars a month. Why? Why were you sending my mother money when no one else around here seemed to care about her?"

"Now look here — "

"Sandi told me that Dan wasn't the only one who didn't get along with Barry McGerrigle. She told me you had some kind of grudge against him, too. What happened? Did you and Dan go in on it together? Did you decide to get rid of him? Did you talk Dan into doing the dirty work, and when he went to prison, you sent a money order to my mother every month to make up for it? Is that what happened?"

"Now look here, kid — "

"Is it?" Mick demanded. It made sense. The two of them had joined forces against Barry McGerrigle in the bar that night. Who was to say they hadn't teamed up to do worse? "Fifty bucks a month! Did you really think that was enough?"

Heck's face grew pale. He grabbed Mick by the arm, his fingers biting deep into Mick's flesh, and dragged him down the alley beside the drugstore.

"Now you look here," he repeated, leaning toward Mick, his breath hot on Mick's face, "I had nothing to do with what happened that night. Leastways, nothing that happened after Dan left the bar. It wasn't me."

Heck's grip grew tighter with every word, until it was all Mick could do not to cry out in pain.

"I sent your mother that money because I felt sorry for her. And because I thought maybe if I hadn't opened my big mouth that night, maybe things would have turned out different. But I got involved in something that was none of my business. I got Dan even more worked up than he already was, and then — " His voice broke off. He shook his head, as if he were trying to clear it. His hand went to his chest. He looked pale and dazed. Or maybe, Mick thought, it was an act, maybe he was trying to avoid answering.

"And then what?" Mick prompted. "What happened?"

118

Slowly, with what looked like tremendous effort, Heck straightened up. He stared at Mick. "Barry McGerrigle got killed, that's what happened," he said, "and I felt sorry for your mother. There she was with a brand new baby and a husband in prison. I did what I could. That's not a crime."

There was something else. There had to be. Why else would crusty old Heck have sent money to Mick's mother when no one else had? He was hiding something. He had to be.

"Dan's coming back for me," Mick said. "And when he does, I'm going to tell him I know about you. I'm going to tell him I know how the two of you conspired to kill Barry McGerrigle. And then I'm going to go to the police."

"Maybe you should just let sleeping dogs lie," Heck said. "Because you never know what they're going to do when they wake up — lick your hand or take a great big bite out of you."

Mick drew himself up straight and tall, so that he was eye to eye with Heck. No rickety old man was going to scare him. "I guess we'll see," he said.

They stood there for a few moments, nose to nose, silent, sizing each other up, Heck seeming to study Mick to take his measure, while Mick was doing his best to look a good five years older than he was.

"You're not going to back down, are you, kid?" Heck said at last.

Mick shook his head. He could be as stubborn as the next guy.

"Well, if you expect anything from me, you're out of luck," Heck said. "I was good and drunk that night. Drunker than a man should ever be. I don't have a good recollection of what happened. I can't tell you anything. Maybe someone else in town saw something, but it wasn't me."

"What do you mean?" Mick asked. "*Did* someone else see something? What did they see?"

Heck shook his head angrily. "How would I know? A man died and your father took responsibility for it, that's all there is to it as far as I'm concerned." He turned away from Mick. Then, slowly, he turned back. "I always did wonder, though. . . " he said. "How did he get there?"

"How did who — " Mick began

"Hey, in there!" someone shouted.

Mick and Heck turned their heads in unison and saw a police officer coming toward them. Mick recognized him. It was Les Culver, the man his mother had once dated.

"What's going on in there?" he said. Then, "Heck Dinsmore, is that you?"

"You can see it's me, Les," Heck snapped.

Les Culver came down the alley toward them. He looked from Mick to Heck. "What are you up to in here, Heck? You bothering this boy?"

"Since when do you have the right to poke your nose into a private conversation?" Heck said. "This is a free country — or it was last time I checked."

"Since when did you start holding your private conversations in alleys?" Les Culver asked.

"That's none of your business." Heck turned and strode away.

Les Culver looked at Mick. "*Was* he bothering you?"

Mick shook his head. He dashed out of the alley just in time to see Heck's battered old truck pull away.

Watching it, Mick wondered what Heck had been talking about. More importantly, he wondered *who* he'd been talking about. He decided to ask Heck later, over at Sandi's. Right now, though, he had to mail Aunt Charlene's contest entry.

Mick's plan was simple. He would mail Aunt Charlene's entry, then he'd hitch a ride out to Sandi's place to resume his conversation with Heck.

The mailing of the recipe went off without a hitch. Then he started to walk down the street, his thumb out to hitch a lift out to Sandi's. Uncle Jim picked him up.

"Don't you know it's not safe to hitchhike?" he said. "Your Aunt Charlene would have a fit if she knew."

"Can you drop me at Sandi's place?" Mick asked.

"I will if you promise I won't ever catch you hitching again."

"Deal," Mick said, although he wasn't sure he meant it.

Five minutes later Uncle Jim turned onto a road that ran in the opposite direction from Sandi's place.

"Uh, Uncle Jim, Sandi lives back that way."

"I know where she lives," Uncle Jim said. "I said I'd take you there and I will. I have a little errand to run first, though. I told Charlie Lewis I'd drop by his place this afternoon to pick up a load of siding, and that's what I intend to do. Then I'll run you over to Sandi's."

Charlie Lewis ran what looked like a junk yard. Charlie himself wasn't there, but a note on his door gave Uncle Jim directions to the siding he'd come for.

"Put these on," Uncle Jim said, producing a pair of work gloves from under the seat and tossing them to Mick.

"What for?"

"So your hands don't get cut up." He grinned.

Grumbling, Mick pulled them on. He wanted to go to Sandi's now, but here he was farther away from her place than he had been when he'd started.

It took over an hour to load the siding into the pickup. Then, because the siding was too long for the truck bed, it took another thirty minutes for Uncle Jim to secure the load.

"Tell you what," he said when they finally left Charlie Lewis's place behind, "you help me unload this and I'll be happy to run you over to Sandi's."

"Uncle Jim — "

Too late. They passed the turnoff to Sandi's and before Mick knew it they were back at Uncle Jim's place.

"Look, I'm in a bit of a hurry — "

"Thirty minutes," Uncle Jim said. "We'll have this unloaded in thirty minutes."

It took a lot longer. Mick's stomach was rumbling for supper by the time they were done. So was Uncle Jim's. He wanted to grab a sandwich. Mick had to hound him for a lift.

They arrived at Sandi's just in time to see an ambulance pull away. Its lights weren't flashing; its siren wasn't wailing. Mick glanced at Uncle Jim, who punched a little harder on the gas pedal. He looked worried.

Sandi was standing on her porch, watching the ambulance as it grew smaller and smaller. Her eyes glistened with tears. Behind her, motionless on a wicker chair, sat Jessie. Her face was pale. Her hands were clasped white-knuckled in her lap.

"What happened?" Mick asked. He was aware of Uncle Jim behind him.

"It's Heck," Sandi said. "His heart."

"Is he going to be okay?" Mick asked. But he knew the answer already. The ambulance had been in no hurry.

Sandi started to sob.

"Why don't you come inside?" Uncle Jim said, his voice gentle. He circled around Mick to catch Sandi under the elbow and help her into the house. "I'll call Charlene."

Mick looked at Jessie.

"I was with him," she said. She spoke each word slowly and softly. "We were out in the back field working. All of a sudden he straightened up and said how hot it was. Then he just keeled over. It's so far from the house, Mick. I shouted, but I didn't know if anyone heard me. I wanted to run for help, but he wouldn't let me." Her eyes clouded with tears. Mick bounded up the steps to sit next to her. He took one of her hands in his.

"When I went over to him, he grabbed me by the

wrist," she said. "And when I told him I wanted to go for help, he just held onto me. Oh, Mick, you should have seen the look in his eyes. He looked so scared, like he knew he was going to die. Then all of a sudden he seemed to relax, like suddenly he wasn't afraid anymore. I thought at first that whatever had happened had passed and that he was going to be okay." She started to cry in earnest now. Mick held tightly to her hand. He'd never been with a crying girl. He wasn't sure what he was supposed to do. After awhile she stopped and smiled wanly at him.

"I'm sorry," she said.

"It's okay."

"He said something just before he died, Mick. He said, 'How did he get there?'"

"What?" It was the same thing Heck had said in the alley. "What did he mean?"

"I don't know," Jessie said. She wiped at her tears with the palms of her hand. "He said it twice and then . . . and then . . ." Her tears began once more and Mick held onto her as best he could, offering what comfort he could.

# Chapter Nine

"I still can't believe it," Jessie said, standing with Mick out by her mailbox. "I've had plenty of time for it to sink in, but I still can't believe that Heck is dead." She shook her head slowly, emphasizing her disbelief. "Has Les Culver managed to locate his wife and daughter yet?"

Mick hadn't even remembered that Heck had a family. "Nobody said anything to me about it. What happened to them, Heck's family?"

"Well, the way I heard it, his wife just up and left him. Took the little girl — she was just a baby, I think — and didn't even tell Heck where she was going. Sandi told me Heck almost fell apart over it. She said she thinks his wife leaving helped Heck to decide to turn over a new leaf. That and my grandfather's death."

Mick wasn't really listening. He was thinking about Heck's last words: "How did he get there?" What did that mean? How did *who* get *where?* It had to have something to do with what had happened the night of Barry McGerrigle's death. Heck had said that something about that night was bothering him. But what? What did it mean?

"Mick? Mick, did you hear me?"

Mick blinked at her.

Jessie sighed and shook her head. "You're off in dream land, aren't you?"

"He knew something."

"Who?"

"Heck. I talked to him earlier — a couple of hours before he died. He started to tell me something about what happened the night your grandfather was killed, but we got interrupted."

Jessie sighed. Her breathing was shaky, as if she were fighting for control. "I guess we'll never know what that was. Poor Sandi. I wonder how she's holding up."

"She was pretty upset last night," Mick said.

"Maybe we should go over there, see if she needs anything."

Mick nodded. They started off together.

Sandi's face was grey. Her eyes had an unnatural sheen to them. She looked as if she hadn't slept all night.

"No," she told them, "no, there's nothing you can do. There isn't even anyone to call. The only family Heck had around here was his cousin, and he died a year ago. I don't think Les has had any luck tracing Emily." Emily, Mick guessed, was Heck's wife. "There's no one to take care of all the details." Tears sprang to her eyes. "No one except me."

"Why don't you try to get some rest, Sandi?" Jessie said.

"I can't. I have to go into town to talk to Mitchell Tremain. He needs instructions for the funeral. There's no one else to take care of any of that."

"Do you want me to call my mom?" Jessie said. "She could drive you."

"No, it's okay," Sandi said. "I can manage it." She hesitated. "There is something, though."

"Name it."

"I'll need his good suit. I think he should be buried in it, don't you?" Jessie and Mick nodded in unison. "It's just that I can't . . . I can't bring myself to go into his room. Do you think maybe you and Mick — ?"

"We'll get it right now," Jessie said. She nodded at Mick, and the two of them left Sandi's kitchen and headed across the yard to the small cabin that Heck had long ago transformed into a cosy home.

The place was small, not much larger than the average-sized living room. But it was as neat as a showroom. The bed was so tightly made there wasn't so much as a wrinkle on the bedspread. The dresser top was dust-free. A stack of *National Geographic* magazines sat in the middle of a small table beside a recliner chair. There were no built-in closets. Heck's clothes were stored in a pine armoire, which Jessie flung open. She sorted through the clothes hung inside and pulled out a dark suit.

"Do you think this is the one she wants?"

"Huh?"

"You're doing it again, aren't you?" Jessie said.

"You're thinking about what Heck knew."

Mick nodded. He knew what Jessie was going to say before she said it.

"Heck can't tell you anything anymore."

Heck Dinsmore's funeral was bigger than Mick would have imagined for a man of so few words who seemed to keep mostly to himself. When he glanced around the interior of the church, Mick saw every person he had ever met in Haverstock, and what looked like every person he hadn't yet had the pleasure of exchanging greetings with. There wasn't a spare stretch of pew in the place.

Sandi was sitting right up front, flanked by a couple of older women Mick didn't recognize. Whoever they were, they sure seemed to care about the old guy, because they all clutched wads of tissue which flew up to their eyes regularly to dab at tears.

After the service everyone piled into cars and trucks and drove across town to the cemetery, where they stood around a little longer while the minister said a final prayer and Heck was lowered into the ground. Then, one by one, the people who had known Heck filed by the open grave and tossed a handful of dirt into it. The procession of cars and trucks headed back across town to the church hall, where the women of the congregation, Mick's aunts among them, served little triangular sandwiches with the crusts cut off, and platters of squares and tarts and cookies.

It was strange, Mick decided, to be part of a

crowd of people who had gathered on the occasion of a death, but who were laughing and gossiping and stuffing themselves with food. His mother's funeral had been a more sombre affair — Mick and his father and a few of his mother's friends from work had met first at the funeral home and then had clustered around the grave in the cemetery. They had dispersed from there. There had been no sandwiches or sweets, no laughter at all.

Mick sat in a corner of the church hall, in front of a plate of food he'd barely touched, and wondered about what Heck Dinsmore had said. Sandi, he thought. She knew Heck probably better than anyone else. Maybe she knew something. Maybe he'd said something to her that might help. His eyes swept the church hall, looking for her. He found her over by the door to the kitchen, leaning against the wall, her face pale, her eyes red from crying. She was talking to Wanda Stiles. This wasn't the best time to pester her about what Heck might have said, he knew, but maybe he could ease around to the subject, not get her too upset. Besides, when would be better? He started across the crowded room toward her, only to be intercepted.

"There you are!" Jessie said. "Mom tagged me for waitress duty. I think I've passed around two dozen trays of sandwiches. My feet are killing me. You want to go outside and get some air?"

"I was just going to speak to Sandi for a minute," Mick said, glancing over toward the kitchen door. Jessie seemed to sag. She looked tired. Tired, and something else besides.

"You knew Heck for a long time, didn't you?" Mick said.

"All my life," Jessie replied. Tears welled up in her eyes.

Mick took the empty tray from her hands and set it onto a nearby table.

"On second thought," he said, "I could really use a breath of fresh air."

They went outside together to sit on the grass and talk.

When he got back inside and looked for Sandi, she was gone. He whirled around, scanning the room for her.

He spotted his cousin Lucy.

"Lucy? Hey, Lucy, have you seen Sandi?"

"She just left," Lucy said. "Mom and Jessie's mom took her home. I heard them say Sandi is exhausted. They're going to put her to bed and make her take one of those sleeping pills Dr. Bertrille gave her."

Mick worked his way through the crowd to the door, and reached it just in time to see Wanda Stile's station wagon pull out of the parking lot. Too late.

*How did he get there?*

How did *who* get *where*?

If the question really had something to do with Barry McGerrigle's death, then Heck had to have been referring to Dan. Dan, who had dumped Mick in Haverstock nine days ago and who had promised to be back in a few days, a week at the most. Mick stared up at the ceiling of his cousin's room and wondered if he'd ever see him again. Where was Dan? What was he doing? And what about that night?

*How did he get there?*

How did Dan get to the hotel? That had to be what Heck meant, because from there he went straight to jail via the road that ran past Barry McGerrigle's place, and there was no mystery about how that had happened. So, how did Dan get to the hotel? Why did that even matter? It was what happened after he got to the hotel that mattered, not what happened before. But Heck had made it sound so important. Or had he? Maybe the fact that those words turned out to be the last he ever spoke to Mick gave them a weight they didn't deserve. Maybe they meant nothing at all. Maybe Heck had been trying to confuse Mick — maybe because Mick had been right in the first place, when he had seen Heck's handwriting on those envelopes. Or, maybe Heck *had* been in on it, and those fifty-dollar money orders amounted to guilt money, paid out in paltry instalments, buying relief of conscience on the cheap. Maybe.

But if the question meant nothing, why was it the last thing Heck had said before he died? Weren't a person's dying words supposed to be important? Weren't you supposed to pay special attention to them?

Mick woke suddenly in the middle of the night. The house was silent. The only sound he heard was the crickets rubbing their legs together in the grass outside. He sat up, listening, registering the time on the clock — one-thirty — and wondering if he could possibly make himself wait until morning. Waiting, he knew, would be best. You just didn't call people you barely knew in the middle of the night to ask them odd questions. He lay down again, but the instant his head hit the pillow he knew that he wasn't going to be able to stand the suspense. He had to know *now*.

As quietly as he could, he crept downstairs to the kitchen and thumbed through the phone book. Only after he'd punched out the numbers and the phone on the other end of the line started to ring did he remember that Arthur Dietrich had a daughter, which meant that he was probably married, which meant that at this very moment Mick might be disturbing the sleep of Mrs. Dietrich.

"Hello?" asked a groggy voice.

"Mr. Dietrich?" Mick whispered. "It's Mick Standish."

"What?" Mr. Dietrich said. "Who is this? Speak up."

Mick repeated his name in a slightly louder whisper. "I'm sorry to bother you so late," he said. "I just wanted to ask you something." Arthur Dietrich said nothing. Mick wondered if he had fallen asleep on the other end of the line. "You said the first will you drew up for my grandmother was a secret. You said she made you swear you wouldn't tell Big Bill or anyone else. Did you keep her secret, Mr. Dietrich? Did you tell anyone about the will?"

Silence on the line.

"Mr. Dietrich?"

"I cannot quite believe," Mr. Dietrich said at last, "that you have actually wakened me from a sound sleep for the sole purpose of questioning my integrity."

"I'm sorry, Mr. Dietrich, but I — "

"I kept my word to your grandmother. For your information, I pride myself on keeping my word. As far as I'm concerned, the terms of that will were a secret. If anyone else knew what the will contained, they did not, I assure you, learn it from me."

"I'm sorry, Mr. Dietri — "

All he heard was a receiver clicking into place over in Morrisville. He hung up the phone, shut off the kitchen light, headed back up stairs, and almost jumped out of his skin when he reached the top.

A figure loomed in the shadows of the upstairs hall, clutching a weapon. A baseball bat, Mick saw.

It was Uncle Jim. He came forward, grim-faced. The bat was still raised, ready to swing. Mick retreated a pace. What the — ? Then Uncle Jim squinted at him.

"Oh, it's you," he said, lowering the bat just a little. "I thought I heard a prowler. You should be careful, Mick. You don't know how close you came to getting whacked over the head."

Mick stood on the stoop of Big Bill's house and rapped on the door frame.

No answer.

He rapped again, more sharply, until his knuckles smarted.

Still no answer.

Mick frowned. The door was ajar, which meant that Big Bill had to be in there. So why wasn't he answering? Pure stubbornness, he thought. Or maybe he'd fallen down. He was on old guy, maybe as old as seventy. What if he'd fallen down and couldn't get up again? What if he'd had a heart attack or a stroke, like what had happened to Heck?

Mick shoved the door open.

"Hello?" he called. "Anyone here?"

He heard a groan coming from the bedroom. He approached the closed door and pressed his ear against it.

"Hello?" Mick called again, softer now. "Hey — " He didn't feel right about calling the old man Big Bill, and for sure he wasn't going to call him Grandfather or Grandpa. "Hey, are you okay in there?"

First there was utter silence. Then the sound of someone — Big Bill — blowing his nose. Then Mick heard footsteps, and the bedroom door flew open. Big Bill came out, his thatch of white hair dishevelled, his eyes red and moist-looking. He wiped at his nose with a crumpled tissue. Mick glanced over the old man's shoulder at the rumpled bed, and the tangled sheets, and, in the midst of the jumble, a gold-framed photograph of a woman. Big Bill turned, following Mick's gaze, and quickly yanked the bedroom door shut.

"Are you okay?" Mick asked again. A stupid

question. It was obvious the old man was far from okay.

"Of course I'm okay," Big Bill said gruffly. "What do you want? Don't people believe in knocking anymore?"

"I knocked," Mick said.

"Well, what do you want?" He was back to his crusty old self, and the vague feeling of sympathy that Mick had had for him vanished like mist under a hot sun.

"I wanted to ask you something about my — " How was he going to express this? How could he avoid speaking the word? "About my grandmother's will."

"Margaret's will? What about it?"

"You knew that in her first will she'd left that property to Dan. You said you were trying to figure out how to raise the subject with her."

"So?" Big Bill said.

"So, you knew what was in her will before she told you."

"Of course I knew. What kind of fool do you take me for? Someone who doesn't know what's going on under his own roof?"

"But you said she kept the will a secret from you," Mick said. "And Mr. Dietrich says he was sworn to secrecy. He says he never told anyone about that first will. So how did you know what was in it? How did you even know it existed?"

Big Bill brushed past Mick and padded into the kitchen in his sock feet. He grabbed the kettle from the stove and turned to fill it at the sink.

"What difference does it make how I knew?" he said. "What's done is done."

"That's for sure," Mick said. "Look — " He was talking to the old man's back, and suddenly that irked him. He needed Big Bill to look at him, to see how much he needed to know. He reached out and touched the old man's arm. Big Bill jumped and spun around.

"What?" he demanded.

"My whole life, I never heard a good word about this place or about the people here," Mick said. "I didn't know my other grandmother was still alive. I never even knew exactly what it was that landed Dan in prison in the first place. It's all been this great big secret, and every time I try to find out what happened, someone tells me a lie." He hadn't meant to say so much to this sour old man, but once he started, he couldn't make himself stop. "I just want to know, that's all. I want to know what happened and why. I know it doesn't mean anything, that nothing's going to change. But I still want to know."

Big Bill set the kettle on the stove and turned up the heat.

"I was always curious about you," he said to Mick. "I don't expect you to believe it, and I can't say I went out of my way to find out, but I did wonder about you. I wondered what kind of kid you were, what kind of man you'd end up being." His face relaxed. He raised a hand and for a moment Mick thought the old man was going to put it on his shoulder, maybe even hug him. But the hand stopped in mid-air, then shifted to Big Bill's head, and scratched it.

"Jimmy told me about the will," he said finally. "Jimmy always likes to keep his ear to the ground. He was a smart kid, the smartest of the three of them. The hardest worker, too. Had to be to get where he is. Buddy had it made — he always knew he was going to get the farm when I retired. Jimmy had to scrape to get ahead. When he and Charlene first got married, they held down regular day jobs to pay their mortgage, and worked on the farm in the evenings, before work in the mornings, all weekend. They put off having kids until pretty late, just so they'd have a fighting chance of staying out of debt. I was glad Jimmy got his grandfather's land. He deserved it. He was second oldest. That may have been the only good to come of what happened, and I can't say I'm sorry for it."

"How did Uncle Jim find out about the will?"

Big Bill shrugged. "I never asked him. Like I said, Jimmy kept his ear to the ground." He opened the refrigerator and brought out a carton of eggs.

"About that other thing . . . " he said slowly.

Mick frowned. "What other thing?"

"When you came in. I'd appreciate it if you didn't mention that to anyone."

He was embarrassed, Mick realized. "No problem," he said.

"Because I wouldn't want anyone to get the wrong impression," Big Bill said.

Wouldn't want everyone to think he had been crying, Mick guessed. "No problem," he said again. Who would he tell, anyway?

"Today would have been our wedding anniversary," his grandfather said. "She was a fine woman. You would have liked her."

Mick nodded. He'd just have to take the old man's word for that.

"Well, I guess I'd better get going," he said.

Big Bill nodded at the carton of eggs. "Have you had breakfast yet?" he asked.

Mick shook his head.

"I'm not much on the fancy stuff," Big Bill said, "but no one can match me on bacon and eggs, sunny side up."

Mick stared at his grandfather. He'd been in Haverstock well over a week, and this was the first friendly gesture Big Bill had made.

"Sounds good to me," he said.

# Chapter Ten

"Sandi? Sandi, are you here?"

Sandi's spotless kitchen was deserted. It looked as if it hadn't been used for days. Mick stood on the gleaming tile just inside the door and listened. The house was silent.

"Sandi?"

Still nothing.

He left the kitchen, went back out onto the porch, and stared out over the yard. No one was out there, either. The entire farm looked abandoned. He started across the yard toward the old barn.

"Sandi?" he called in at the door. "Sandi, it's me, Mick!"

"In here!" a voice called back. Sandi's voice. Mick stepped into the barn, blinking to adjust to the gloom inside.

"Over here," Sandi said.

Slowly, like an instant photograph developing before his eyes, the darkness of the barn's interior began to form itself first into shadows, then into outlines, until finally the shape that was Sandi emerged, standing directly opposite him, loading a wheelbarrow with brown flowerpots.

"Need a hand?" Mick asked.

"I *always* need a hand." She smiled, but there wasn't much enthusiasm behind the expression, and when he got close to her, Mick saw that there were dark smudges under her eyes. "Every year I put dozens of herbs into pots like these," she said. "I don't know why, but potted herbs are a popular item at farmers' markets. People could just as easily grow their own, but they don't. I guess I shouldn't complain, though. It's money in the bank for me."

Mick helped her fill the wheelbarrow full of pots, then trundled it out to the yard where they spread the pots on a trestle table she had set up. He filled the bottoms of the pots with soil. Sandi planted each with herbs from flats she had been growing — basil, thyme, sage, parsley. For awhile they worked in silence, as Mick tried to decide whether to ask her what was on his mind. She looked as though she hadn't slept since Heck's funeral, and he felt bad about raising painful memories.

"Ever since Heck died," Sandi said, "I've been wondering what I'm going to do. It's a lot of work to run this place. More than I can manage on my own. But at the same time I can't imagine taking on another partner — not after all these years with Heck. Besides, I don't even know who'd be interested. This place is a living, but a person will never get rich here. That didn't bother Heck, though. He wasn't interested in money, not after Emily left."

"Emily — that was his wife?"

Sandi nodded. "She was a lot younger than Heck, and she had no patience for the way he was leading his life back then."

"Drinking, you mean?"

Sandi sighed. "He tried to stop, but he didn't manage it until after Emily left with the baby. I thought his heart would break. Funny, you'd think something like that would drive a man *to* drink, but with Heck it was the opposite. He sobered up. I think he believed Emily would come back one day, and he wanted to be ready when she did."

"But she didn't."

"Heck never saw her again. Never had contact with his daughter, either. She was barely two when Emily left town with her."

Mick filled another few pots with soil and passed them to Sandi. "I talked to Heck the afternoon he died," he said after a few moments.

Sandi's eyes misted. She smiled softly. "He liked you. He said he saw a lot of your father in you. He liked your dad, too."

"He . . . he said something was bothering him about the night Barry McGerrigle died."

"He did? What?"

"He didn't say exactly. He just said, 'How did he get there?'"

Sandi frowned. "How did *who* get there? Get where? What are you talking about, Mick?"

"Not me," Mick said. "Heck. He said, 'How did he get there?' I don't know what he meant. I was

141

going to ask him about it, but I never had the chance. I was wondering if maybe you had any idea what he might have meant."

Sandi shook her head.

"I thought he might have meant, how did Dan get to the hotel that night," Mick said. "It's the only thing that makes sense, but I still don't get it. Why would it matter how Dan got there? The important thing is how he left, and everyone knows that. He left with Uncle Jim."

"He left in the 'Vette," Sandi said. She paused in her re-potting. "You should have seen that car when he first brought it home. What a piece of junk! It had been sitting out behind a barn over in Morrisville for over a decade. He bought it for next to nothing, then spent the better part of two years pouring every dime he could lay hands on into parts for it, and every minute of time he could grab away from chores to fix it up. He had it in pretty good shape by the time he was finished. I won't say it looked brand new, but it came pretty close. Until the accident, that is. Going up over that concrete divider didn't do it much good."

The picture Sandi conjured up was hard for Mick to visualize — serious, hard-working Uncle Jim tooling around town in a vintage Corvette.

"I thought he spent all his spare time on his farm," Mick said. "That's what he told me. He never mentioned anything about a Corvette. Is that how he managed to snare himself a wife?"

Sandi looked at him in surprise. "I don't think your mother was the type to be impressed by fast cars. The Corvette belonged to your father, Mick. I was talking about Dan, not Jim."

"Dan and Uncle Jim left the hotel in Dan's car?" Sandi nodded.

"You said you called Uncle Jim to come and get Dan, so I assumed they left the hotel in Jim's car," Mick said. "But they didn't. They left in Dan's car."

"That's right," Sandi said.

Now Mick was confused.

"Then Dan must have arrived at the hotel the same way, in his own car. So there isn't any mystery about how he got there."

"I guess not," Sandi said.

"Then what was Heck talking about? Did something happen to Dan on the way *to* the hotel? Is that what he meant?"

Sandi said she didn't know. Mick struggled to hide his frustration. Sandi was feeling bad enough without having to work side by side with someone in a bad mood. But he'd been so sure that what Heck had said was some kind of clue to what had really happened, and now that had turned into a dead end. Nothing made sense.

"Maybe he picked up somebody on the way to the hotel," Jessie said. She had arrived at Sandi's at mid-morning, and was helping Mick transfer more herbs into pots while Sandi sat at a small table on the porch, lettering labels with a calligraphy pen.

"Even if he did, why would that be important?" Mick asked. "What would it have to do with how or why my father killed your grandfather?"

143

Jessie had no answer. "Maybe Heck was talking about something that happened before that night, something that might have led up to it," she said. "After all, he didn't actually say, 'How did Dan get to the hotel on that particular night?' did he?"

"Well, no," Mick admitted. "I just assumed . . . " He thought back to what Heck had said in the alley. "He didn't actually say that 'there' was the hotel, either." That was what was so frustrating. Heck hadn't been specific about anything — not the time or the place or . . . "He didn't actually say he was talking about Dan, either," Mick said slowly.

"Who else could he have meant? You said you were talking to him about Dan, didn't you?"

"Yes," Mick said. "But we know how Dan got to the hotel. He drove there in his own car. He left in the same car." He stopped abruptly. "How far is it from here to the hotel?"

"Eight kilometres. Maybe ten. Why?"

But Mick was already striding across the yard to the porch where Sandi sat with her labels and her pen. Jessie hurried to catch up with him.

"What about my Uncle Jim?" Mick asked. "How did he get to the hotel that night?"

Sandi looked up from her lettering, a puzzled expression on her face.

"The night of the accident," Mick prompted her. "You said you phoned my Uncle Jim to come down to the hotel and get Dan. How did he get there?"

"In his truck," she said.

"Did you see it?"

"Mick, I'm not sure I'm following — "

"Did you see Uncle Jim's truck that night?"

Sandi looked at him like he was crazy to be obsessed about such a trivial thing, but then she nodded. "When I looked outside and saw Jim and Dan fighting, Jim's truck was there. In fact, that's how I saw the two of them so well. The truck headlights were shining on them."

"What about after?"

Sandi looked confused. "After?"

"If Uncle Jim drove from his place to the hotel in his truck, and if he drove back in Dan's car, then he must have left his truck parked outside the hotel. Did you see it?"

Sandi shook her head.

"You didn't see it?"

"I didn't see it because it wasn't there," Sandi said. "I locked up about an hour after Dan and Jim left — after we all heard what had happened. Heck was back by then and looking for a place to sleep. Emily didn't like him showing up at home when he'd been drinking. I said he could bunk at my place. We went out to the parking lot together and Jim's truck wasn't there. I remember walking across the lot to my car. I remember quite clearly that mine was the only car left in the lot."

"Maybe Mr. Standish picked up his truck when he came back into town with the police," Jessie said.

Sandi shook her head. "The police station is right across the street from the hotel," she said. "I saw the two police cruisers outside, and I saw Ed Hanley's tow-truck with Dan's Corvette hooked up to it. I remember that. But there were no other cars around. Not a one."

"You're sure?" Mick said.

Sandi nodded. "I'm positive. I remember looking at the 'Vette and thinking how sad it was that all that work Dan had done had ended up in such a bad way — killing a man. And then I saw Jim come out of the police station with Les Culver and they got into one of the police cruisers and drove off. I assumed Les was taking Jim home. Or to Big Bill's place to tell him and Margaret what had happened. Jim's truck was nowhere around."

"You're absolutely positive?" Mick said.

Sandi nodded.

"What, Mick?" Jessie asked. "What are you thinking?"

"Just that Uncle Jim didn't walk to the hotel that night."

"Which means," Jessie said slowly, "that someone must have driven him. Charlene, I guess, if he came from home."

Mick looked south across Sandi's field to Uncle Jim's farm.

"If it's okay with you, Sandi," he said, "I'm going to knock off early. I have a few things to take care of."

"Want me to come with you?" Jessie asked.

Mick shook his head. "Sandi needs help," he said. "I'll call you, I promise."

Aunt Charlene was alone in the house. She wore rubber gloves and was kneeling on several layers of newspaper, scrubbing the interior of the oven with an old rag. She looked up when Mick entered the kitchen, and wiped a wisp of hair out of her eyes with the back of her wrist.

"Where's everyone else?" Mick asked.

"Lucy and Penny are at 4-H. Jim went into town to run a few errands. Is everything okay, Mick? You looked flushed."

"I — I ran over from Sandi's place."

"From Sandi's? On a day like today? You must be parched. Here, can I get you — "

"I need to ask you something, Aunt Charlene," Mick said.

She sat back on her feet and waited.

"Where were you the night Barry McGerrigle died?"

She laughed. "You sound like the detective in a murder mystery," she said.

"I'm serious, Aunt Charlene."

She frowned. "What do you mean, where was I?"

"Dan was down at the hotel. When he'd had too much to drink and started making trouble, Sandi called Uncle Jim to come down and get him. Where were you?"

"I was here."

"When Sandi phoned?"

She nodded.

"And then you drove Uncle Jim into town so he could get Dan," Mick said, stating this as a fact, not posing it as a question. "Then what happened?"

Aunt Charlene thrust the blackened rag into a bucket of water and wrung it out. She refused to meet his eyes as she asked, "What do you mean, what happened? I drove home again."

"I mean before you came back home. After you saw the two of them argue outside the hotel." Mick felt confident now that he was on the right track. She hadn't denied driving Uncle Jim into town, nor was she denying having witnessed the fight. She *had* been there. Maybe she had seen more than Sandi had. "You were in the truck outside the hotel. The truck headlights were shining on Jim and Dan while they argued. Then you saw Dan get in behind the wheel of the Corvette."

Aunt Charlene stared down at the black depths of the bucket of water. She said nothing.

"I know you saw what happened, Aunt Charlene." He didn't actually know. He was guessing. But maybe he could trick her into revealing something. "I know why Uncle Jim didn't come forward and tell the whole story. And I guess in a weird kind of way I can understand that. But what I don't understand is why *you* didn't come forward, why you didn't tell the truth. You didn't have anything to be afraid of."

Aunt Charlene's face turned pale. "I don't know what you're talking about, Mick."

"I think you know exactly what I'm talking about. All this time you've known what happened that night and you haven't said a word. Now I know what happened. I want everyone to know the truth, Aunt Charlene. It isn't right that something like that happens and the truth is hidden." He didn't add that all the lies he'd been told had made it even worse.

Now she looked nervous. "The truth was never hidden," she said. "Dan confessed, didn't he? He pleaded guilty. Jim said Dan grabbed the wheel. He said Dan wrestled control of the steering wheel from him and shoved his foot across and onto the gas. If Dan hadn't done that, Barry McGerrigle wouldn't have died that night and everyone knows it."

Mick stared at his aunt in stunned silence. "You're telling me," he said slowly, scarcely believing it, "that Uncle Jim was driving that night? Uncle Jim and not Dan?"

The rag fell from Aunt Charlene's hand. "You said you knew," she whispered. "I thought . . . "

"Uncle Jim was driving Dan's car when Barry McGerrigle was killed," Mick repeated slowly. "Uncle Jim and not Dan."

# Chapter Eleven

Aunt Charlene struggled unsteadily to her feet. She hauled the bucket of dirty water to the sink and slowly emptied it. Then she began to gather and fold the newspaper that had been spread on the floor.

"Sandi says Dan was driving when his car left the hotel," Mick said. "Now you're telling me that Uncle Jim was driving?"

Aunt Charlene spun toward him. "I'm not telling you anything, Mick," she said. "This conversation is finished."

Mick shook his head. She might think there was nothing more to say, but as far as he was concerned, the conversation was just beginning.

"Uncle Jim told me Dan was driving. Why would he say that if it wasn't true?"

Aunt Charlene slammed the oven door shut, and carried the empty bucket and the dirty rag out onto the back porch. Mick followed her.

"Arthur Dietrich also told me that Dan was

driving. You remember him, don't you? He was Dan's lawyer. Big Bill and Uncle Buddy tell the same story. Everyone but you says that Dan was driving. Why is that? Why hasn't anyone else mentioned that it was Uncle Jim who was driving the car that night?"

"I'm not talking about this anymore," Aunt Charlene said, her voice tight. "Leave me alone, Mick." She squeezed by him.

Mick followed her back into the house and up the stairs. She ducked into her room and closed the door in his face, but it would take more than a slab of wood to get rid of him. "It seems to me that anyone telling the whole story about what happened that night would make it clear who was driving," he half-shouted through the door. "Up until now, I thought there were only two people who knew the whole story — Dan and Uncle Jim — and the way they both told it, Dan was driving." At least, that was the way Mr. Dietrich said that Dan had told it. Dan had never discussed the matter with Mick. And then there was Sandi — Sandi had seen the car drive away with Dan behind the wheel.

"Now you say that Uncle Jim was driving. There's only one way you could know that for sure. You followed the car, didn't you, Aunt Charlene? You followed it and . . . then what? You saw them make a switch? You saw Uncle Jim get behind the wheel? Did you see what happened after that, Aunt Charlene? Did you see Barry McGerrigle get hit?"

From beyond the door, he heard his aunt stifle a sob.

"I'm not going away, Aunt Charlene, and I'm not going to let this rest. My whole life I've been told one thing — that my father was an innocent man. Then I come here and I find out that's not true, that he pleaded guilty to taking another man's life. I've heard all kinds of stories about what happened. And now they turn out to be lies, too. Or at least half-truths, which amounts to the same thing. I'm not going to give up until I find out the truth. So if you won't tell me what you know, I'll have to go to the police and ask them to figure this out for me. I'm sure they'll be very interested, because from what you've told me, I wouldn't be surprised if they didn't know who was really driving that night, either."

The door flew open. Aunt Charlene wiped the tears from her eyes. "You don't want to stir this up, Mick," she said. "It's not what you think. It won't do anyone any good."

Mick stared at his aunt. This was obviously upsetting her, and he was sorry about that. She'd been nicer than anyone else in Dan's family. But he couldn't back down, not now.

"Tell me what you know," he said. "Everything."

She shook her head.

"Tell me the truth, Aunt Charlene. Please."

She looked down at the floor.

"Please, Aunt Charlene. I *have* to know."

She stared at him, then started to speak slowly, like a shy child reciting a poem.

"After Sandi called, I drove Jim to the hotel," she said. "I dropped him off and he told me to go home. He said he'd make sure Dan got to Bill and Margaret's safely, and then he'd be home. But when I turned the truck around in the hotel parking lot, I saw the two of them arguing. They were fighting over the car keys. Jim was trying to wrestle them away from Dan. For a minute it looked like he was going to win. Dan was pretty unsteady on his feet. He'd had a lot to drink. Then all of a sudden the fighting stopped." She paused and looked up at Mick. "They just stood there, frozen, staring at each other. I don't know why. I guess Dan must have said something that hit a nerve. He had a knack for doing that, for finding just the right button to push to make Jim explode. He must have done it that night because all of a sudden Jim threw the keys at Dan and then he waved at me. He wanted me to get out of there. As I pulled away from the hotel, I saw Dan get in behind the wheel of the Corvette. The car was just starting to move forward when Jim jumped into the passenger seat."

She got a faraway look in her eyes as she continued. She spoke like she was a play-by-play commentator describing the action to him exactly as she was seeing it.

"I killed the truck lights and pulled around a corner. I was worried that with Dan driving in the shape he was in, something bad was going to happen. And I guess I was mad at Jim, not so much for letting Dan drive, although there was that, too, but for getting into the car with him. I was mad at him for taking such a chance with his own life, especially then."

"What do you mean, especially then?"

"I was pregnant at the time," Aunt Charlene said.

Mick frowned. If his aunt had been pregnant fifteen years ago, then . . .

"I lost the baby," she said quietly. "The day after the accident . . . after Barry McGerrigle was killed, I went into labour prematurely." Her eyes clouded. "Things didn't work out." She drew in a deep breath. "Anyway, I was worried about what might happen, so I followed Dan's car at a distance, with the truck lights off."

In response to Mick's puzzled expression, she explained: "Back in those days, when Jim told me to do something, he expected it to get done, without any argument. He'd sent me home. He would have been angry if I'd followed him. That would have shown that I doubted his control over the situation. Frankly, I did doubt it. Jim's temper gets the best of him sometimes. And Dan was driving erratically. I was worried. After a minute or two the car pulled over and Dan got out and went over to the ditch. I could see he was throwing up. Then he got in the passenger seat and Jim took the wheel. I can't tell you how relieved I was. Everything was going to be okay. I thought that with Jim driving nothing bad could possibly happen. I dropped back even farther and kept the lights off — I didn't want Jim to think I was second-guessing him. I was really surprised when he made that turn-off down the road that ran by the McGerrigle place."

"Why surprised?" Mick asked. "That road runs directly to your place, doesn't it?"

Aunt Charlene nodded. "But it's the long way home," she said. "Not by much, but that route adds a minute or so to the trip. Anyway, I decided to stop following him at that point — there was obviously nothing to worry about. I decided to take the shortcut so that I'd get back home before Jim. Then I heard this terrible sound." Her gaze wavered. She looked back down at the floor. When she finally looked up again, her eyes were filled with tears. She struggled to keep them under control.

"I knew something had happened," she said. "I made the turnoff and turned on my lights, and in the distance I could see Dan's car on the wrong side of the dividers that ran down the middle of the road. When I got there, Barry McGerrigle was lying in a pool of blood. Dan was unconscious in the front passenger seat. His mouth was bleeding. Jim was just about in shock. He told me that when Dan saw Barry on the road, he grabbed the wheel and jammed his foot onto Jim's on the accelerator and the next thing Jim knew the car was flying over the divider and Barry was hit."

Mick thought over these new facts in silence.

"I was pretty hysterical," Aunt Charlene said. "Jim sent me home. He told me he'd take care of everything. When Jim finally did come home, he told me that he'd told Les Culver that Dan had been driving."

"What?" Uncle Jim had admitted to Aunt Charlene that he had lied to the police?

"He told Les that Dan was driving," she repeated. "He said that Dan was drunk and that he was driving and that he'd run down Barry McGerrigle by accident. I argued with Jim about that. I knew it wasn't true. But Jim told me that if he told Les what had really happened, Les would know that Dan did it on purpose. Dan would be charged with murder. This way, he said, if Dan played his cards right, he could plead to a charge of manslaughter. Maybe he'd get a lighter sentence that way. The important thing, Jim said, was that it would be too hard on his mother if she thought Dan had killed a man on purpose. It was bad enough to have done it accidentally. Margaret was very sick at the time. Jim was afraid something like that would kill her.

"I didn't like it," Aunt Charlene continued. "I didn't think Jim should be lying for Dan, or for anyone else, for that matter. And I was nervous about what Heck would say — "

"Heck? How does Heck come into this?"

"I saw him," Charlene said. "His cousin had a place on the other side of the road from where Barry was killed, an old barn. Some people said it was a smugglers' hideout, but I don't know, there was never any proof of that, it was just something people said. Anyway, I was pretty sure I saw Heck on the other side of the road, and I was pretty sure he'd seen what had happened. I said so to Jim."

"And?"

"And he told me not to worry about it. He said Heck was fall-down drunk that night and that he'd already told Les that he hadn't seen a thing. Still, I was worried. What if Heck remembered something the next day? But Jim told me that wasn't going to happen, and that I should forget about it. The next day I went into premature labour. I was rushed to the hospital and my baby . . . I lost my baby." Aunt Charlene shook her head. "I don't really know what happened after that except that Jim said there was no need for me to be involved in any of it. I was very sick. I'd lost a lot of blood and I was so depressed. Jim wanted to protect me, I guess."

"But don't you think there might have been a lot more questions if people had known it was Uncle Jim, not Dan, who was driving that night?" Mick said. "Haven't you thought about it yourself, Aunt Charlene? Haven't *you* wondered?"

"Wondered about what?"

"You said Uncle Jim was driving. So it was Uncle Jim who decided to make the turnoff down the road that runs by Barry McGerrigle's place. Why did he do that?"

"I don't understand — "

"Everyone knew that Barry McGerrigle was out on that road walking his dog every night at eleven o'clock. Jessie told me it was common knowledge. Uncle Jim must have known he'd be out there that night. So why would Uncle Jim take that route when he knew Barry would be out there and when he had Dan in the car beside him, and still mad at

Barry? Plus, it was the long way home. You said so yourself. Why would Uncle Jim choose that particular route on that particular night?"

"What are you saying?" Aunt Charlene asked, her voice sharp. "Are you trying to blame this on Jim somehow? He had nothing to do with it. Dan and Barry got into a fight in the hotel that night. A dozen people saw them. They'd been feuding for weeks. Who knows why Jim took that road home? What does it matter? The point is, he did, and when Dan saw Barry out for his walk, he grabbed the wheel and steered for Barry and as a result Barry was killed. It was Dan who did it. Dan was responsible. Jim had no reason to hurt Barry. Dan did. Besides, Dan confessed. He pleaded guilty."

Mick stared at his aunt. She was a good woman. He didn't doubt that she believed what she was saying. But there was so much she didn't know. The question was, how much did he want to tell her when what he said might hurt her?

If he told her what he knew, she might see it for herself. She might understand exactly what must have happened that night. And if she did, the next step would be for her to tell the police what no one had revealed to them all these years.

But if Mick told her, and if he was right, wouldn't he be doing to her exactly what Uncle Jim had done to Mick's own mother? Wouldn't he be dooming her to the same life his own mother had led? She, too, would be the wife of a man in prison, and her children, his little cousins, would have to put up with what he'd endured for so long.

Could he really do that to them, to her?

There was an important difference, though. At least, there was if he was right. If it had happened the way he now was sure it had, then, unlike Mick's mother, Aunt Charlene wouldn't be the wife of a man wrongly convicted. She'd be the wife of a murderer.

Mick peered into her eyes, red from crying. He had to tell her. He couldn't stay quiet.

"Aunt Charlene, what if I told you that Uncle Jim had as good a reason to want Barry McGerrigle dead as Dan did — maybe an even better one?"

Aunt Charlene shook her head. When she spoke, she no longer sounded defensive. She was angry. "That's ridiculous. Jim didn't have anything against Barry. Not a thing. Look, Mick, I understand that it's hard for you to be here. It must be painful to find out so much about your father. I don't like to criticize, I liked your mother, really I did, but I think it might have been wiser if she'd told you the truth right from the start. I guess I can understand why she didn't, though. She was probably trying to spare your feelings. But you have to face facts, Mick, and the facts are that your father had a grudge against Barry McGerrigle, he had a reputation for being wild, and he confessed to what he did. What happened, happened. It's not going to do anyone any good — least of all you — if you try to blame it on someone else. Now if you'll excuse me, I should see to supper."

She stood tall now, and brushed by Mick on her way to the stairs. Mick watched her until she reached the bottom, half of him believing she was right — Dan *had* confessed, he'd stood up in front of a judge and had accepted responsibility for the death of another man. But did that make it true? What about the facts that hadn't come to light fifteen years ago, the niggling little facts that had been swept under the carpet and had lay hidden from sight ever since?

"Maybe Dan *was* mad at Barry McGerrigle," Mick called down to her. "Maybe he was even mad enough to want him dead, although I can't see one man killing another for a few dollars in back wages. But Jim had his reasons, too."

Aunt Charlene whirled around and looked up at him from the bottom of the stairs, her face pale and round, like a lump of dough.

"I've had enough of this," she warned. "There was no bad blood between Jim and Barry."

"But there was between Jim and Dan," Mick said.

She was silent.

"Jim was expecting to inherit his mother's land, wasn't he? She was terminally ill, and he was sure that when she died he'd get the land."

"Which he did."

"Under the terms of her *second* will, not her first one."

"If you're referring to the fact that Margaret revised her will after what Dan did, so what? No one was surprised that the land went to Jim in the end."

"Maybe not," Mick said. "But from what I hear,

they *were* surprised that she'd left the land to Dan in her first will."

Her face reddened. She knows I'm right, he thought. But all she said was: "So?"

"So, that will was supposed to have been a secret," Mick said. "Arthur Dietrich drew it up and he says she made him promise not to tell anyone about it. But it looks like the secret didn't stay secret, even though Mr. Dietrich says that as far as he knows, Margaret didn't tell anyone about that first will."

"Mick, I'm getting really tired of this."

"Uncle Jim knew." He paused to let the words sink in. "I don't know how he knew, but he did. Big Bill told me that Margaret never said a word to him about that will. He found out from Uncle Jim that she was going to leave that land to Dan. Uncle Jim told him *before* Barry McGerrigle died. You know what I think? I think that when Jim found out about that will — "

"He went out and killed Barry McGerrigle?" Aunt Charlene seemed horrified that he was making such a suggestion.

"He took advantage of an opportunity to get Dan out of the way," Mick said. "To put him in a bad light. To make Margaret think so badly of him that she'd change her will. He must have felt he deserved that land far more than Dan did."

"That is so ridiculous it's not even worth discussing," Aunt Charlene said. "You were right when you said that there are only two people who really know everything that happened that night, and that's the two people in Dan's car. If Jim did what you're suggesting — and believe me, I'm not saying that he did; the idea is preposterous — but if he did, why would Dan plead guilty? Why wouldn't he tell the truth?"

"You said yourself he was unconscious when you got to the car."

"He was unconscious because Jim hit him. Jim was so angry, so shocked, that he hit Dan and knocked him out."

"How do you know that?"

"Jim told me. His knuckles were red and sore when he came home that night."

"How do you know Jim didn't hit Dan beforehand?"

"Really, Mick!"

She shook her head again and turned away to go to the kitchen. Mick watched her and debated with himself how much more to say. It was clear that she loved Uncle Jim and believed him. If he went on, if he told her everything he knew, he would hurt her, maybe badly. But if he stopped now, he would never know the truth.

"Dan was blackmailing Uncle Jim."

She didn't even flinch, but disappeared through the doorway into the kitchen.

"Uncle Jim was having an affair and Dan found out about it and threatened to tell you." Mick followed her, talking to her back because she kept turning away from him, getting potatoes from under the sink, carrots from the bottom of the fridge, turning back to the sink. "Uncle Jim paid him off so he wouldn't tell you. I'm positive that's what they were fighting about in the parking lot that night when Uncle Jim was trying to get the keys away from Dan. Dan threatened to tell you about Uncle Jim's affair. That's why Uncle Jim suddenly quit fighting with him. That's why he let Dan drive."

She turned the water on in the sink and started to peel the potatoes.

"Maybe that was the last straw," Mick said. "That would explain why after Dan got sick and Jim took the wheel, he all of a sudden decided to take the long way home. He knew Barry McGerrigle would be out there walking his dog. It was common knowledge. He also knew that everyone had seen Dan and Barry McGerrigle go at it in the bar that night. There were a few other things he knew, too, things that he knew weren't common knowledge — like the fact that he was being black-mailed, and the fact that his mother had decided to leave her land to Dan, not him. Maybe he went a little crazy. Maybe he all of a sudden saw the perfect chance to solve all of his problems. All he had to do was kill Barry and then tell Dan, If you don't shut up about my affair, I'm going to tell everyone you ran Barry down on purpose. It would be Jim's word against Dan's, and everyone knew Dan was drunk and angry, and everyone knew Jim was sober and responsible and didn't have any grudge against Barry. The trouble was, there was someone else around. Two someones Jim hadn't counted on. Heck, who was too drunk to be sure

163

what he saw. And you. Uncle Jim had to make up a story for you. And you believed him."

She didn't turn, but over the sound of the running water he heard her say angrily, "Dan pleaded guilty."

"He pleaded guilty to manslaughter. He probably didn't think he'd get much time. He probably thought that the judge who would hear the case would be Delbert Johnson, Big Bill's friend, a guy who had known Dan all his life. Everyone thought Dan had a good chance of getting off easy. Even his lawyer thought so. He probably would have, too, if Delbert Johnson hadn't excused himself from the case."

The only response he got was the water running. She didn't believe him.

Okay, Mick thought. It couldn't be helped. He'd have to actually say it. "The woman Uncle Jim was having an affair with," Mick said slowly, "her name was Helen Sanderson."

The water was still running, but the potato Aunt Charlene had been peeling fell from her hand. She turned to face him. There were tears in her eyes.

# Chapter Twelve

"I don't believe you," Aunt Charlene said, raising a hand to wipe a tear from her cheek.

But if she didn't believe him, why was she crying? And why had she looked so stunned when Mick mentioned Helen Sanderson's name?

"You have to come with me to the police," Mick said. "If I'm right, Dan didn't do anything wrong."

"If he didn't do anything wrong, why did he say he did? Why did he jump at the chance to plead guilty to manslaughter?"

That was the one thing Mick didn't understand.

"Maybe the police can figure that out," he said. "Come on, Aunt Charlene. We have to go into town."

"I don't think so, Mick."

Mick stared at her. "You can't keep quiet. You have to tell the police what you know."

"What I know is what my husband told me. Dan grabbed the steering wheel. He killed Barry McGerrigle. He did it on purpose and he's lucky he had a brother who was willing to lie for him or he might still be in prison. Is that what you want me to tell Les Culver, Mick? Because that's what happened."

The tears had dried on her cheeks. She was holding tight to the back of a kitchen chair.

"If you don't tell the truth, Aunt Charlene, I'm sorry, but I will. The police will come to you if you don't go to them. You'll have to tell."

Aunt Charlene stood her ground. Her soft blue eyes hardened into ice. She looked as immovable as the silo standing out behind the barn.

"I thought you were different from the rest of them," Mick said. "I thought you cared. I guess I was wrong."

He turned away, not wanting to look at her anymore, not wanting to see her again. He stormed from the house, telling himself he was never going back. He would walk all the way into town, he would tell the police everything he had found out, and then he would see if Sandi would lend him enough money for a bus ticket home where he would wait for Dan.

The walk took longer than he thought and hurt his feet a lot more than he imagined they would. By the time he reached town, every muscle in his thighs and butt ached. His mouth was as dry as the dirt on the shoulder of the road, and he promised himself that the first thing he would do when he left the police station was buy himself a soda — make that two sodas — ice cold. But first he had a job to do.

166

"Mick! Hey, Mick!"

He turned and saw Jessie on the sidewalk across the street. She waved, then darted toward him.

"Hey, where have you been? I phoned your aunt over an hour ago, but she said she didn't know where you were. What's happening? You promised to call me. Is everything okay?"

"Yeah," Mick said. "Yeah, sure." He was barely listening to her, his eyes and his attention were on the police station just down the street. "Look, I have to talk to Les Culver — "

Jessie peered at him. "You found out something, didn't you? You want me to come with you?"

"No," Mick said quickly. Maybe too quickly. The words came out sounding like he didn't want her around, didn't appreciate her help. "I just . . . I have to talk to him alone, okay? Why don't you go over to the café and get yourself a cold drink. I'll be over as soon as I can to fill you in."

She hesitated and looked at him uncertainly. "Are you're sure you're okay?"

Mick nodded.

"You promise to come over to the café when you're finished?"

"Promise," Mick said.

She nodded. "Okay. I'll be waiting." She reached out and squeezed his hand. "Don't take too long, okay?"

Mick's skin was warm where she had touched him. He looked into her moss green eyes and wondered what it would be like to walk down the street holding her hand.

"Mick? Did you hear me?"

"Huh?"

"I said, don't take too long, okay? I want to know what's going on."

"Okay," he said, but instead of rushing to Les Culver's office right away, he stood on the sidewalk to watch her cross the street, and didn't turn away until she had disappeared into the café.

Les Culver was sitting at his desk, rooting through a drawer and swearing softly to himself. His service revolver was lying on the corner of his desk, beside an oily rag. He must have been cleaning it, Mick thought. He wondered how often Les was called on to fire the gun, wondered if he'd ever fired it.

"I know you're in there somewhere," Les Culver muttered. He glanced up and looked suddenly sheepish, when Mick stepped into the office and swung the door partly shut. "I had a couple of candy bars stashed in one of these drawers," Les explained. "At least, I thought I did. If I were pressed to conclude where they had got to, I'm afraid I'd have to suspect Constable Andrekson. That boy's got a worse sweet tooth than me — and a misguided belief that the contents of my desk constitute department property instead of private property." He slammed the desk drawer shut. "What can I do for you, Mick?"

"I want to talk to you about Dan."

Les arched an eyebrow and leaned back in his chair. "That so? What about him?"

"You were called out that night, weren't you?" Mick said. "The night of the accident."

"Accident?" Les Culver shrugged. "You mean the night old Barry McGerrigle bought the farm?" He chuckled. "That's a little rural humour." He thought a moment, then pulled open another drawer and rummaged through it. "Yeah, I was called out there. Why are you asking?"

Mick wasn't ready to answer that question yet. "What kind if shape was Dan in when you got there? Was he conscious?"

"Conscious and nursing a pretty sore jaw, as I recall," Les Culver said. "Your Uncle Jim let him have it after what he did."

"Where was he sitting?"

"Sitting?" Les Culver looked up from the drawer he was rooting through, a baffled expression on his face. "Nobody was sitting anywhere when I got there, son," he said. "They were standing — that is to say, Jim and Dan were. Old Barry, he was lying on the side of the road."

Okay, nothing there. "Who told you what happened? Jim or Dan?"

"Jim."

Aha! "Didn't you find that odd, Uncle Jim telling you what had happened when it was supposedly Dan who had been driving and who had run down Barry McGerrigle?"

"Not really," Les Culver said. "Dan was pretty groggy. He'd been drinking. He'd been hit pretty hard. And, if you ask me, he was in shock over what he'd done. Jim told me what happened, we brought

Dan in, and the rest is a matter of public record."

"What if I told you it didn't happen the way you think?" Mick said.

That finally succeeded in capturing all of Les Culver's attention. He closed the drawer he had been pawing through and leaned forward in his chair.

"Is there some point you're trying to make here, Mick?"

"It was Uncle Jim who killed Barry McGerrigle, not Dan."

Mick wasn't sure what kind of reaction he had been expecting. Incredulity, perhaps. Astonishment. Shock. He got none of these from Les Culver. Instead, the police officer leaned way back in his chair and slowly shook his head.

"There were only three people out on that road that night," he said to Mick. "One of them is dead, one of them stood right up there in court where everyone could see him and took responsibility for that death — and you know who I'm talking about, son — and the other is your Uncle Jim. Are you telling me that fifteen years after the fact, your Uncle Jim suddenly confessed to you that he's a murderer? Because that's the only explanation for you coming in here now and telling me such a crazy story." He paused and peered closely at Mick. "Well, I guess there is one other possibility," he said.

Mick held his breath. Was Les Culver going to listen to him? Was he going to help Mick uncover the truth at long last?

"I suppose," Les Culver said, "that it's possible that you're psychic or something. That's the only other way I can think of that you can be so sure what happened out on a dark country road before you were even born. Of course, since you've got the story all twisted around about who was driving and who did what, I guess that would make you a pretty bad psychic."

"What about Heck?"

"What about him?"

"He was there that night, wasn't he?"

"Yeah," Les Culver said, "he was there. But he was as drunk as a skunk. Told me so himself before he scurried away."

"He saw what happened."

"Told you that, did he?"

"He was going to."

"Uh-huh." The officer shook his head again. "In other words, Heck didn't tell you what happened?"

"He would have," Mick said. "He told me something about that night bothered him."

"And you concluded that something had to be that your Uncle Jim killed Barry McGerrigle. Killed him and framed his own brother for the crime. Is that about the size of it?" He made the idea sound ridiculous.

Mick nodded.

"Well, well, what do you think of that, Jim?"

He spoke as if Jim were right there in the room with them, which he wasn't. It was then that Mick saw the chess board on the little table behind Les's desk. A few of its men lay scattered around it, evidence of a game in progress.

Mick whirled around. Uncle Jim, two take-out coffees in his hands, stepped through the half-opened doorway into Les's office.

Mick peered at him. When had his uncle entered the station? How much had he overheard?

"Well now," Uncle Jim said, shaking his head and sounding sad. "You take a kid in when his own father won't have him. You put a roof over his head and good home cooking in his belly. And what do you get? Not so much as a thank you. No sir. What's the matter with you, Mick? Did your mother do such a bad job bringing you up that you can't even be grateful? Why try to blame me for something your own father admitted to doing himself?"

Uncle Jim, in his blue jeans and his checked shirt, forearms tanned as brown as tree bark, cheeks ruddy, eyes piercing blue, looked about as crooked as a cornrow, and no more dangerous than a baby calf. But he had been driving the car that night, and the story he'd told Aunt Charlene was different from the one Dan had told Arthur Dietrich.

"If you've been standing out there the whole time listening, then you know what I think," Mick said. "I don't know how you got Dan to say what he did, but the fact is, you were driving the car that night and you had the most to gain from Barry McGerrigle's death. If he hadn't been killed that night, your mother would have left that land to Dan, not you."

Uncle Jim threw back his head and laughed as

if he'd just heard the world's funniest joke. When he finally stopped, he said, "Can you prove it?"

Mick looked into his uncle's eyes. There was no hint of amusement in them.

"Can you?" Les Culver asked.

Call my Aunt Charlene, Mick wanted to say. Ask her. Except that Aunt Charlene wouldn't tell the truth. Which meant that the only thing Mick could do was recite the facts as he knew them. Uncle Jim had a motive. Two motives, in fact. First, Dan was blackmailing him. Second, Uncle Jim had found out that Dan was going to inherit his mother's land, land that Uncle Jim believed should go to him instead. While Mick explained, Les Culver looked sharply at Uncle Jim, and Mick thought for a moment that he was making some headway.

"You're not taking this seriously, are you, Les?" Uncle Jim said. "Come on, you know me. You've known me all your life. And you know Dan, too. Are you really going to listen to this crazy story?"

Mick pressed on. Dan was driving when he and Uncle Jim left the hotel, but they switched a few minutes later after Dan got sick. When the car turned down the old highway that ran behind the McGerrigle place, it wasn't Dan who was driving, but Uncle Jim. Uncle Jim chose the route home. Uncle Jim knew where Barry McGerrigle would be that night. Uncle Jim had run him down.

"Ridiculous," Uncle Jim said.

Mick concentrated on Les Culver. "Think about it," he said. "At first Dan insisted he didn't remember what happened. He didn't change his story until later, *after* Uncle Jim visited him in jail. How could a guy who'd had so much to drink that he couldn't remember running into someone right after it happened, all of a sudden recall the details clearly enough to confess?" He thought he saw something change in Les Culver's face. Les looked at Uncle Jim, his face folded into a question mark.

"Of course he was drunk," Uncle Jim said. "He'd been swilling beer all night. That's why he ran Barry down. He was drunk and crazy."

Les looked at Uncle Jim for a long time, then he turned back to Mick. "Look, son — "

"Ask my Aunt Charlene," Mick said. He wasn't sure what she'd say, but maybe Les Culver could ferret the real story out of her. "She knows Dan wasn't driving. She knows it was Uncle Jim behind the wheel of the car when Barry McGerrigle was hit. She knows how dazed Dan was. He was probably passed out when it happened."

Les Culver frowned. "Charlene was there?"

"She told me she was," Mick said. "She's the one who told me Uncle Jim was driving. Go out and see her. Ask her yourself."

"He's crazy," Uncle Jim said. "Charlene was home that night. You know she was, Les. You saw her yourself when you drove me home."

"How did you get down to the hotel that night to pick up Dan?" Mick asked. "Aunt Charlene drove you."

"She drove me and then she went straight home."

"She drove you and then she followed you because she was worried that with Dan driving, you'd get hurt. She saw the car stop. She saw Dan get sick. She saw you take over the wheel. She was surprised when you decided to go by Barry McGerrigle's place on the way home. That's the long way home, isn't it?"

Les Culver was looking at his best friend with new interest. "Is this true, Jim?"

"No, it's not true." He grabbed Mick by the elbow. "I've had enough of your nonsense, Mick. Come on. I'm taking you home."

"If you don't mind, I think I'll tag along," Les said. "I'd like to ask Charlene a few questions."

"You can't be serious," Uncle Jim said.

Just then the phone rang. Les picked up the receiver and identified himself. Then, mostly, he listened, with only an occasional, "I see," and "Oh?" When he hung up, his face was sombre. He looked at Uncle Jim and said, "That was Charlene. She was crying."

"Crying? Why? What's happened?"

"She says she wants me to come out to the house. She says she wants to talk to me about the night Barry McGerrigle died. She also said something about Helen Sanderson. You want to tell me what's going on, Jim?"

Uncle Jim said nothing. His normally ruddy face went as white as paper. For a moment he seemed paralysed. Then he said, "I have to go now," and started for the door.

"Now hold on there a minute, Jim," Les Culver said. He reached Uncle Jim in two long strides and grabbed him by the arm. "I think you'd better — "

One minute Les was standing up straight, in control of the situation, the next minute he was crumpled on the floor, stunned by a blow from a fist.

"Don't," Mick said as his uncle reached for the doorknob. He scooped Les Culver's service revolver off his desk and aimed it.

Uncle Jim turned back to him. He smiled when he saw the revolver in Mick's hand. "What are you planning to do? Shoot me?"

Mick gripped the revolver with both hands and tried to look as determined as he could. He hoped his uncle wouldn't notice that he was trembling. He'd never even held a gun before. He wasn't sure there were even bullets in it. Even if there were, Uncle Jim was right: what was he going to do, shoot? Still, he couldn't let Uncle Jim walk out that door. If he did, his uncle would run, he was sure of it. He'd have to, because Aunt Charlene had already admitted to Les Culver that what he'd been told all those years ago wasn't the truth. No, he couldn't let his uncle go. Mick glanced down at Les Culver on the floor, willing him to wake up and take charge of the situation. But Les Culver didn't stir.

"Put the gun down, Mick," Uncle Jim said.

Mick held fast. "I won't let you leave. I can't."

Uncle Jim shook his head. He still had a smile on his face as he came toward Mick, hand outstretched. "Give me the gun, Mick, before someone gets hurt."

Mick held fast, even as his uncle's hand reached out to him.

"Let go of the gun, Mick."

Mick couldn't. "You killed Barry McGerrigle," he said. "You killed him and somehow you managed to hang it on Dan. You ruined his life, Uncle Jim. You stole that land from him. You stole my mother's husband from her. You made sure I didn't have a father. I can't let you walk out of here. No way."

"Is that so?" Uncle Jim said. His hand closed around Mick's, and Mick felt the gun being pulled away from him. He scrabbled for a better hold, Uncle Jim tried to push him away, but Mick held fast, determined not to let his uncle do anymore damage. It had to stop. The lying and covering up had to stop right here, right now.

Then, like a cannon, the gun went off. Mick looked down at the revolver now in Uncle Jim's hand. It was such a small thing when you really looked at it, but it made a sound like thunder. Mick's knees buckled. He saw red — blood — then black, and he thought, so this is what it's like to die.

# Chapter Thirteen

The first thought that swam into Mick's pain-fogged mind was: Uncle Jim. What had happened to Uncle Jim? Had he got away? The next was: Where am I? He forced himself to focus. He was in a hospital. But *how* am I? What happened? Why does it feel like I've been cut in half by a flaming sword?

Then: What about Les Culver? Was he all right? Had he been badly hurt? Was he even alive?

He closed his eyes, and the world spun faster and faster around him until he was out of control, whirling out into space, revolving at double time in inky blackness. When he opened his eyes again, it was because he was being stabbed in the side, skewered through with a red-hot blade. He awoke with a scream in his throat, and found himself looking into the interested face of a man he had never seen before. A doctor. Behind him, Les Culver, looking a little pale, but very much alive. Mick felt a wave of relief wash over him.

The doctor lifted the sheet that covered Mick, pulled aside the gown Mick was wearing, and lifted the gauze over the spot where Mick burned.

"Looking good," he said, and grinned at Mick. "You're a lucky kid. An inch or two in the other direction, and your intestines would have been torn apart. And, let me tell you, that would not have been a pretty sight. Not to mention what it would have done for your prognosis."

Les Culver's face hovered above Mick again.

"Can I talk to him now?" he asked the doctor.

"Don't see why not," the doctor said. "I'll check in with you again a little later. And don't worry," he said to Mick. "I can pretty much guarantee you that you'll be out of here tomorrow, day after at the latest." He flashed another toothy grin and disappeared from the room.

Les Culver dragged a chair up to the side of the bed and dropped down onto it. "Well, well," he said, shaking his head and leaning so far forward across the railing of the bed that Mick could feel his warm breath on his face. "Who knew you'd turn out to be an archaeologist."

Mick frowned. What was he talking about?

"You've been digging up the past," he said. "Re-opening fifteen-year-old cases. Solving them."

Uncle Jim! "Where's Uncle Jim?"

"In lock-up," Les said. "I never thought I'd see that day. You have any idea what it's like to throw your best friend into a jail cell? You have any idea what it's like to think your best friend may have committed cold-blooded murder?"

Best friend? No. Father? Mick said nothing. Then, "What about Aunt Charlene? Is she okay?"

"She made a statement. She's pretty upset. She says she feels like a fool for not having seen the truth years ago." Les Culver looked deep into Mick's eyes. "I know how she feels. I thought I made all the right moves. A couple of people saw Dan behind the wheel when his car left the hotel that night. A lot more people saw him good and drunk. There was serious thought given to whether the charge should be homicide or manslaughter. He was a wild kid, Mick. He had a reputation. It wasn't much of a stretch to believe he'd do something stupid."

The pain in Mick's side was so sharp, so intense, that he had to fight the urge to cry out.

"It bothered me a little," Les said. "Kind of niggled away at me. I remember thinking, how can a guy be so drunk he can't stand up, can't even remember being in an accident, how can a guy like that have been capable of driving in the first place? I wondered about it, but I shoved it out of my mind because — well, because of your father's reputation. And because your uncle told me that's what had happened."

"And because you didn't like Dan?" Mick asked.

Les Culver met his searching gaze straight on. "That, too." He looked down at the floor for a moment. "Your aunt also told me that she saw Heck Dinsmore out there that night. Like your dad, he was pretty drunk, and more than a little reluctant to talk to me since he'd just paid a visit to his cousin's barn."

"What was so special about his cousin's barn?"

"The border's not far from here. Alf Dinsmore was running a little smuggling operation back then. Heck didn't want to let that particular cat out of the bag. The next morning, when his head had cleared a little, he headed down to my office to talk to me. Apparently your Uncle Jim dissuaded him."

"How do you know that?" Mick asked.

"Your uncle told me. After you were shot, I guess he realized he had no way out. He's the one who called for help for you, you know. When I woke up, the ambulance was there and your Uncle Jim was making them take care not to hurt you when they lifted you up onto the guerney."

Mick's head started to spin. The pain shot up his side. Maybe he was fine, like the doctor said. Maybe he'd be ready to be discharged from the hospital tomorrow. But right now the pain cut as sharp as a freshly honed knife. He closed his eyes, telling himself he needed to rest for a minute. Just for a minute. And then he would ask Les Culver what was likely to happen next.

He didn't open his eyes again until the next morning. The pain in his side was still sharp, but he didn't feel so woolly headed, and he was ravenously hungry.

"Well, look who's awake," said a voice.

Mick looked over at the door to the room and saw a woman in white with a tray in her hands. A tray of food. Mick struggled to sit up, and winced with pain.

"Here," she said, "let me help you." She deposited the tray on the bedside table and used the button control to raise the head of his bed. Then she fluffed the pillows under his head. "There," she said, "isn't that better?"

He nodded gratefully.

"Are you hungry?"

Another nod.

She wheeled the little table over, angled it over the side of the bed to position it in front of him, and lifted the cover off the tray. Never before had a bowl of cereal looked so appetizing. Even the boiled egg sitting in a little cup made his mouth water. He dug in.

"I'm no doctor, but I'd say you're definitely feeling better today," the nurse said.

Mick grinned happily and shoved a piece of buttered toast into his mouth.

"You have visitors," the nurse went on. "One of them has been here since first thing this morning. Do you want to see them?"

One of them had to be Jessie. Mick nodded.

The nurse smiled and left the room. A few moments later, Jessie and Sandi appeared. Jessie's face was knotted with concern when she first came through the door, but as soon as she saw Mick sitting up and eating, she seemed to relax.

"It's true," she said. "You're really okay. I thought . . . Oh, Mick, when I heard you were shot, I was so scared."

"The doctor says I can probably go home tomorrow." As soon as he spoke the words, he felt a hurt sharper than the one in his side. Home. What did that mean anymore?

Jessie sat down on the chair beside his bed and peered into his eyes for a few moments.

"I have some news for you," she said softly. "About your father."

Mick pushed the food tray away. Suddenly he wasn't hungry anymore. He looked from Jessie to Sandi and back to Jessie again.

"What about him?" he asked.

Jessie unfolded the newspaper she was carrying and held it out to Mick. He saw that it wasn't the local weekly, but a daily newspaper from the city.

"Page seven," she said.

Page seven. The ache in Mick's heart eclipsed the searing pain in his side. Dan was in the news. Whenever that happened, it was never good. He'd seen Dan's name in the paper twice before, in the crime digest section. Man arrested . . . Man sentenced . . .

"Here, let me find it for you," Jessie said when Mick made no move to take the paper from her. She spread her arms wide to unfold the paper, then folded the paper back down to a manageable size and handed it to Mick. "Right there," she said.

He had to force himself to look at the brief item. Car Theft Ring Smashed, the headline ran. He scanned the few paragraphs. Police had infiltrated and then broken up a major car theft ring, but none of the criminals was mentioned by name. How did Jessie know this article had anything to do with Dan? He frowned.

"I don't understand," he asked.

"Mick, your father was involved."

"Terrific," Mick said glumly.

"I think what Jessie means," Sandi says, "is that your father was involved in helping the police break up the theft ring." She pointed to a line halfway down that referred to a tip from an informant. "Les spoke with the Metropolitan Police," she said. "Your father was key to those arrests. He even saved a police officer's life in the process. You should be proud of him, Mick."

Mick stared at the few paragraphs of text. When he looked up again, Jessie was smiling at him.

"It looks like your dad's some kind of hero," she said. "Pretty amazing, huh?"

Where was he? Mick wondered. When was he planning to return to Haverstock?

"Les found out about this when he called the police in the city to see if they could locate your father," Sandi said. "He wanted to tell Dan what had happened here."

"And?"

"And they said they couldn't get hold of him."

Disappointed, Mick sank back against the pillow and let the newspaper fall from his hands.

"Apparently," Sandi said, "he's on his way here."

Dan appeared two hours later, exploding into the room, striding over to the bed, grasping Mick by both shoulders, the closest thing to a hug Mick had ever had from his father.

"Are you okay, Micky?" he said. "If I'd known —

When I brought you here, I knew it wasn't going to be easy for you. But I didn't want those creeps to try to get to me by threatening to hurt you."

"Creeps?" Mick said. "You mean, the car thieves?"

Dan nodded. "I had to stash you somewhere where you wouldn't be in danger if things heated up." He smiled wryly. "That's a joke, I guess. I leave you here to keep you safe and my own brother shoots you. I'm sorry, Mick. If I'd had any idea something like this might happen, I never would have brought you here. I should have left you with those people, what's their names . . . the architect guy?"

"Mr. Davidson."

Dan nodded. "He would have looked after you. You never would have got hurt around him."

Mick stared at the man standing beside his bed. Dan Standish. Mr. Screw-up. The man who had spent almost more time in prison than he had out, and all because of something he hadn't even done. "I'm fine," he said. "The doctor says it's not serious."

"He says you were lucky," Dan amended. "Seems like you're a chip off the old block after all, eh, stirring your relatives up so bad they start shooting at you?"

Mick smiled. "Did Les Culver tell you what happened?"

Dan nodded. "It's hard to believe Jimmy would have done that to me," he said at last. "I knew he thought I was a pain in the butt. But to frame me for murder?" He shook his head.

"I don't understand," Mick said. "Why would you plead guilty to something you didn't do?"

For a few moments Dan sat in silence, slowly shaking his head.

"Why didn't you stand up for yourself when it happened?" Mick asked. "Why didn't you tell the truth?"

Dan sighed. "The truth?" he said. "The truth was that I didn't know what the truth was. I remembered getting into the car. I remembered tearing out of that hotel parking lot going about ninety. At least, it felt like I was going that fast. I don't remember anything after that. Jim told me what I'd done. He told me I'd better be straight about it, tell the police exactly what had happened — that I'd got drunk and ran over Barry McGerrigle by accident. He said he and the whole family were sick and tired of the way I was behaving, getting into trouble all the time, and that if I didn't take responsibility for what I'd done this time, if I tried to weasel out of it, he'd tell them I had killed old Barry on purpose. He'd say it wasn't an accident, it was murder." He shook his head again. "He sat right there in the cell with me and he told me, 'It didn't look like an accident to me, Danny. If anyone were to ask me under oath, I'd have to tell them the truth — that it looked to me like you did it on purpose.' He told me, though, that if I could prove that I'd learned my lesson, if I took responsibility for what I'd done, he wouldn't have to be put under oath."

"You mean, if you pleaded guilty to manslaughter, he'd keep his mouth shut?"

Dan nodded. "I thought he was saving my bacon by letting me plead to a lesser charge. I was actually grateful to him for bailing me out after all the trouble I'd given him over the years. And now it turns out he was the one who did it, he killed Barry McGerrigle."

Mick nodded.

Dan stood up abruptly and strode to the window. He looked out for a moment, then spun around to face Mick. His eyes glistened with tears.

"I wish your mother was still alive," he said. "She always refused to believe I'd done what I confessed to. She said I couldn't possibly have done it, I wasn't that kind of person." His laugh was bitter. "I loved your mother, Mick, but there were times when I thought maybe she was a bigger fool than I was, believing a drunk who couldn't remember a thing instead of believing my sober, responsible big brother."

Mick nodded. He knew exactly how Dan felt.

Dan grabbed a tissue and blew his nose. Mick had never seen him so upset.

"I told you what happened here," Mick said. "Now I want to know what happened back in the city. How did my father end up such a big hero?"

The word father felt strange in his mouth — he couldn't remember the last time he had spoken it — and Dan gave him an odd look.

"It's a pretty boring story," Dan said. "You sure you want to hear it?"

"Positive," Mick said. "Every word."

"Well," Dan said, "it all started when this guy I

knew from prison started putting pressure on me. He wanted me to get involved with some guys he knew . . . "

Mick leaned back against his pillow, listening as Dan unfolded his story. Wishing, too, that his mother was alive to hear it.

Three men, standing on the gravel of Big Bill's driveway, hands in their pockets. One of them, Uncle Buddy, kicking idly at the gravel with the toe of his work boot. A second, Big Bill, rocking back and forth, heel to toe, heel to toe. The third, Dan, squinting off past the other two, past the little house, down to the ribbon of river glinting in the afternoon sun.

"I'm sorry about Jim," Dan said.

They were the last words Mick would have chosen if he'd been in Dan's place. There was nothing to be sorry about — except that Jim had lied for so long and Aunt Charlene, the only one who might have changed the way things had unfolded, had had her judgement clouded by her devotion to her husband.

"Do you think Charlene's going to be all right?" Dan said.

"I expect she will be," Uncle Buddy said. He didn't even glance at Dan when he spoke.

Dan nodded. He looked at Big Bill. "Well," he said, "me and the kid had better shove off. Thanks for looking after him." He stuck out his hand, wanting to shake Big Bill's. Big Bill looked at it for a moment, then, not concealing his reluctance, allowed his own hand to be clasped.

"It was Jim who took him in," he told Dan. "Jim was the one who kept an eye on him."

Mick couldn't stand it anymore. They were still treating Dan like he was some kind of criminal, like somehow everything would have been better if he hadn't returned.

"Jim's a murderer," he said to his grandfather and his uncle. "Jim ruined everything for my parents."

"Now, Mick — " Dan said. He laid a calming hand on Mick's shoulder.

Mick shook it off. He didn't wanted to be calmed. He didn't want to shut his mouth and smile and pretend Uncle Jim was really a good guy.

"My mother never believed Dan did anything wrong," he said. "Maybe if you'd had half the faith she did, things would have been different. Did you ever think of that?"

The two men, virtual strangers, stared blankly at him, then looked away again, one back down to the gravel at his feet, the other up at the sky as he rocked back and forth, heel to toe.

Dan squeezed Mick's shoulder. "We'd better get going," he said. "We've got a long drive back."

They started for Dan's car and were just about to get in when a pickup pulled into the driveway. Sandi and Jessie got out, smiling. Dan smiled back, and Mick realized he'd never seen his father look so happy. He wore the same pleased expression that he had last night, when Sandi had invited them to supper at her place. Afterwards they had sat out on Sandi's porch and talked. Well, Sandi had done most of the talking. Dan had leaned back on the porch swing, watching her and smiling, just like he was doing now.

"I brought you some sandwiches for the ride back," Sandi said, and handed Dan a brown paper bag the size of a suitcase. "Also some cake and some fruit," she said, and when Dan laughed, she blushed and said, "It's a long trip."

"Not too long for you to want to make it yourself some time, I hope," Dan said. "I'll show you all the sights."

"I might just take you up on that," she said.

Mick turned from them to Jessie.

"I'm going to miss you, Mick Standish," she said.

"It really isn't as far as Sandi makes it out to be. You can come and visit, too."

"And you can come back here. I know Sandi would let you stay at her place."

"Come on, Micky," Dan said. "We better shove off."

Mick nodded, but he didn't want to leave. Jessie took his hand, led him to the car, and opened the door for him. Then she leaned up and kissed him lightly on the cheek. He felt light-headed as he slipped into the passenger seat.

"It really isn't that far," Jessie said again.

Dan turned the key in the ignition. As he put the car into gear, he glanced at Mick.

"I know things have been pretty messed up over the years, Micky," he said. "But things are going to be better from here on in."

Mick nodded. "I know they will, Dad," he said.

Norah McClintock's most recent novel, *The Body in the Basement,* has been nominated for the Red Maple Award and the 1998 Arthur Ellis Award for Crime Fiction. Her earlier mystery, *Mistaken Identity,* won the 1996 Arthur Ellis Award. Many of her novels have been published internationally.

Although she has a full-time job as an editor, Norah still manages to find time to write. "I love to write because I love to read," she says. "When I was young it cost ten cents to get a library card — I've never encountered a better bargain than that."

Norah lives with her family in Toronto.